ELLA RAE, AMATEUR HORSE RUSTLER!

It had all seemed so simple when Ella Rae
worked it out in her head. She had the map of
the barn where Dark Victory's stall was located.
All she had to do was sneak up there at night
and borrow the stallion for a few hours. Then
the red mare could have a foal, and Ella Rae
would make it up to the Puckett-Smythes by
working extra hard and not taking any pay till
she'd earned the $3,000 stud fee.

But when she got Dark Victory out of his stall,
he had a few ideas of his own about what he
wanted to do. And he quickly expressed himself
in a loud, clear bellow that woke everyone for
miles around, and sent Mr. Puckett-Smythe
racing right smack toward Ella Rae's hiding
place. . . .

*"Very funny, good characterizations . . . will find
a delighted audience of young readers"*
—VOICE OF YOUTH ADVOCATE

More Great Fiction from SIGNET VISTA

~THE~
MONEY CREEK MARE

PATRICIA CALVERT

A SIGNET VISTA BOOK

NEW AMERICAN LIBRARY

TIMES MIRROR

PUBLISHER'S NOTE

This novel is a work of fiction. Names, characters, places, and incidents are either the product of the author's imagination or are used fictitiously, and any resemblance to actual persons, living or dead, events, or locales is entirely coincidental.

NAL BOOKS ARE AVAILABLE AT QUANTITY DISCOUNTS WHEN USED TO PROMOTE PRODUCTS OR SERVICES. FOR INFORMATION PLEASE WRITE TO PREMIUM MARKETING DIVISION, THE NEW AMERICAN LIBRARY, INC., 1633 BROADWAY, NEW YORK, NEW YORK 10019.

RL 4/IL 5+

This is an authorized reprint of a hardcover edition published by Charles Scribner's Sons, a Division of Scribner Book Companies. The hardcover edition was published simultaneously in the United States of America and in Canada—Copyright under the Berne Convention

SIGNET VISTA TRADEMARK REG. U.S. PAT. OFF. AND FOREIGN COUNTRIES

REGISTERED TRADEMARK—MARCA REGISTRADA

HECHO EN CHICAGO, U.S.A.

SIGNET, SIGNET CLASSICS, MENTOR, PLUME, MERIDIAN AND NAL BOOKS are published by The New American Library, Inc., 1633 Broadway, New York, New York 10019

First Signet Vista Printing, January, 1983

1 2 3 4 5 6 7 8 9

PRINTED IN THE UNITED STATES OF AMERICA

FOR GEORGE,
MY BEST FRIEND

Chapter 1

ON THE FIRST day of summer Rosanne Carmody packed her suitcase and left Money Creek, Missouri. She told me she did not plan to come back. Ever.

She dangled her right arm out the window of an old blue truck loaded with chickens. Her long fingernails were painted redder than a rooster's comb. It was her favorite color. "Red is like life," she loved to say. "It's the color of fire and sunsets and fresh beginnings." I wondered which one of her movie magazines she'd lifted that line out of.

Those magazines were on the seat beside her the day she left. Their pages were ragged from being read so often. Her straw church hat lay across her knees. The driver of the truck—she'd met him only an hour earlier when he stopped by The Diner for a piece of warm gooseberry pie (which I'd made myself that very morning) —seemed astonished. All he stopped for was pie. He never figured to catch himself company all the way to California.

"Babe, I just can't stand it anymore," was how she explained it to me. "What I mean, Babe, is that I don't aim to. I hate this no-account country, I hate The Diner, and most of all I hate those darn, dumb horses." She drummed her fingers against one of her magazines.

1

"Which don't mean, of course, that I don't love you a bunch."

"That's okay, Rosanne," I said. "I understand how you feel. I do. Really." I wasn't as sure about it as I pretended to be. Except she was leaving, and it was too late to sit down and have a long talk about it.

"I'll send for you, Babe. I will. Promise. Maybe for Buster and Chloe, too. You first, though, on account of you're the oldest and never needed much tending to anyhow. I'll write, too. Every day."

"Once a week'll be fine with me, Rosanne."

It was one thing for her to write if she wanted to. Every day, if it suited her. But I sure hoped she would not take it into her head to fire a bus ticket into an envelope and send it to me, for I had no intention in the world of ever leaving Money Creek myself.

The fact was that the measure of hate my mother, Rosanne Carmody, had for Money Creek, Missouri, was almost the same size, shape, and color as my love for the place. "Just a wide spot in the road," Rosanne liked to complain. "Nowhere, U.S.A.," she'd groan when she was in a real bad mood.

No way, José, I'd say to myself when she carried on like that. Why, Money Creek had The Diner. It had Buster and Chloe and me. It had Cash Carmody and all his horses—slow ones and eager ones and every kind in between.

Cash raced his little band of mudrunners on weekends and the Fourth of July and Labor Day at fairs all up and down the state of Missouri. Once in a while he even made a few dollars. And if a person could roll fine Missouri names like Blue Springs or Chilhowee or Sugar Creek off the tip of her tongue, why would she take a notion to leave for a place called Hollywood? Nashville,

2

maybe, where the music was good, but California? It never made a lick of sense to me.

Rosanne never let me forget she hated horses. Well, everyone in Money Creek who wasn't dead or stone deaf knew the name of that tune. She sure sang it often enough. "Oh, my god, Cash, not another horse! We don't even have that new TV paid for yet!" she shrieked when Cash brought home the Money Creek mare. "Lord, lord—not another horse!"

Why she insisted the lord had a hand in it was a mystery to me. We all could plainly see that it was Cash himself who'd fetched the critter home. But for some reason, the appearance of that particular horse on that particular afternoon unhinged my mother, Rosanne Carmody. I can date you a tubful of strange events from the moment Cash hauled into our yard with that dark red mare in the back of his truck.

"See you, Babe!" Rosanne cried in my ear, and snatched me from my reverie. She wagged a blood-tipped finger under my nose. "I'll get a job in California and send for you real quick, hear? Don't worry a speck about that, Babe. Promise?" No sooner did she make up her mind than the whole thing seemed to make her anxious.

"Promise," I promised, and waved right back. The blue truck churned up a mighty fog of yellow dust as it careened out of the yard. The chickens in the back exclaimed their opinion on leaving Missouri; it was just about the same as mine. When the truck got to the corner, it turned and squirted up the highway toward St. Louis and the Interstate like a bar of soap along a shower floor.

I blew Rosanne a kiss but she couldn't catch it. She already had her nose in one of her movie magazines. If that truck driver ever got over his surprise at catching company and figured to get some conversation out of her, he might have another think coming—unless he could trade her a juicy piece of gossip about some famous movie person, which, being a trucker and on the road all the time, I doubted seriously he could do.

I tried to see it from Rosanne's point of view. "Babe," she'd told me only a week before, "I'm going to be thirty my next birthday. My life is going by. Only I'm not living it. Other folks are doing that for me. You. Buster and Chloe. And Cash. Most of all, Cash—with his dopey horses and all that talk about laying hands on a fast one." She had sighed and stared out the window of The Diner.

"Those gals in my magazines aren't one bit better looking than me, Babe," she'd mourned. "Only they're having what folks nowadays call growing experiences. Those gals get to go nice places and wear pretty clothes. I'd like to have a life of my own, Babe. A life of my own . . ."

Was it vanity that made me feel I'd been born into the world older than either Cash or Rosanne Carmody? Sometimes I felt ancient. Old as the hills. Like I'd been around forever. What a puzzle it'd always been for me to locate my proper place in the family when I felt like practically the oldest person in the house. You could say I'd been my parents' daughter—but hardly ever their child.

Rosanne figured life had played a mean trick on her. She never told me so right out, but I wouldn't have been mad even if she had. After all, she was only fifteen years old when I came down the road. "I carried you under my heart for nine months," she told me when I was eight and it was Buster who was on the

4

way. You'd have thought in nine months she might've gotten used to me. But I surprised her in ways I never meant to.

"I thought I'd get a boy for sure," she told me. "I was going to name him Clancy." *Clancy . . .* ? Even at fifteen she'd had some peculiar notions. "Only I got you instead—and you were so old. *Old*! Right from the minute you saw the light of day. You put me to shame, Babe. Seems like you were always more grown up than me." I never meant to be—even if I did come into the picture sooner than she wanted.

Besides, she didn't have to explain to me about my beginning. In Money Creek, population 1,813 if you counted everybody in the cemetery, being an expert on your own history isn't hard. Chatter about folks' beginnings, middles, and ends takes lightly to the tongue.

By the time I was six, I knew a woods' colt was a child born before its mama and daddy got around to being married. Once in a while, someone would see fit to remind me I was one—a woods' colt. Except I never could convince myself it made me any less than what I knew myself to be.

Once, when Rosanne and I walked home from a visit to her sister Beatrice's house, we passed by Racker's Mill. It was getting on toward evening, and Rosanne pointed out to me a patch of mossy stuff that covered the banks of Money Creek. It was thick as a quilt, and was stitched all up and down with tiny purple flowers. Bird's-foot violets, she called them.

"It was just such a place where you were begot," she said.

"Oh, Rosanne," I cried. "I'm glad you told me. . . ." She'd been so young! Not much older than me. Only fifteen. Maybe she'd loved Cash then, and he'd loved her, too. What they'd done probably had not seemed wicked and sinful to them. Or likely to invent a person everyone else would call a woods' colt.

I reached for her hand. She allowed me to squeeze her fingers but did not squeeze mine back.

Just the same, in the blue stillness of that summer evening when I was fourteen, Rosanne Carmody must've loved me a little to tell me I'd been begot on a bed of violets. Maybe she did. You never know. It's hard to tell about love sometimes.

When the dust from the blue truck settled back into the road and the clamor of the chickens died away, I could hear Buster and Chloe. They were still in The Diner, crying their hearts out. Rosanne hadn't let them come outside to tell her good-bye. They took things too hard, she said. It was true. They were little; the whole scene was an alarm to them.

I hustled indoors so they wouldn't take it into their heads they'd been abandoned altogether.

Rosanne bailed out on us in such a hurry she hadn't even wiped off the counter. And my, hadn't she packed that little suitcase of hers in a hurry! It was cardboard, made up to look like alligator hide. Soon as you hefted it, though, you knew right off it was only cardboard.

Thinking on it while I wiped the counter clean of coffee rings and gooseberry pie crumbs, I wondered if she hadn't had it packed for a long time. Had her stack of movie magazines collected in a pile in the corner of her bedroom, just waiting for the chance to split out of Money Creek.

Chloe and Buster hugged my knees hard enough to topple me, caterwauling, yellow strings trailing from their red noses. I mopped at them with paper napkins I snatched from a dispenser on the counter, and dabbed at the sweat on their foreheads.

"Quit looking at me like you'd just been invited to an orphans' picnic," I said. "And I'd take it as a favor if you'd quit that infernal yapping."

Buster was in no frame of mind to take advice from anyone. Least of all me. "No, it's you just better hush up, Ella Rae," he howled. "If there's one thing worse in this whole world than mama going off, it's being left here with you." To Buster, Rosanne had always been mama.

Buster's true name was Elvis Presley Carmody, and he wore a pair of steel-rimmed glasses somebody'd left on the counter at The Diner and never came back for. Buster and I didn't have what Mrs. Davison in my Family Life class at school called a good sibling relationship. What we had instead, she told me, was lots of rivalry and hostility.

"You're the meanest person in Money Creek, bar none," Buster rattled on. "It's my bad luck mama didn't take a notion to tuck me right in the back of that ol' truck and haul me all the way to California with her." He paused. "Only I can't stand the smell of chicken poop."

"Well, for being so choosey about your travel accommodations you get to stay here with me," I said. "Here—haul these coffee grounds out back and dump them in the trash barrel. You might as well start to earn your keep around here. Nobody's gonna have time to wait on you anymore. We three will have to run The Diner all by ourselves now."

"I ain't helping you run The Diner, neither!" Buster yelped. "I got plenty to do without taking orders off you. Fact is, Chub Murphy wants me to go catch min-

7

nows with him tomorrow.'' Greed got the best of him, though. I saw one blue eye narrow shrewdly behind the dirty lens of his glasses. "What you fixing to pay me?" he demanded.

"Board and room."

"Board and room? What's that?"

"Means you get your meals to eat and a clean bed to sleep in for free."

"But I already got that!" he hollered in my ear. Buster never spoke in normal tones. Buster hollered, howled, and yelped his way through life. His eyes behind the fly tracks and peanut butter smudges on his glasses were red-rimmed and spiteful. "Board and room ain't enough, Ella Rae. I want real money."

"Real money I don't have. Board and room is what I got and it's my final offer. While you think it over you might as well haul those coffee grounds out back like I told you."

He slammed the screen door behind him—the same screen door I'd patched with nylon fishing string after that little stray dog, Lutie, drilled a hole in it the morning she thought she saw a coon across the road. I could hear Buster sniffle all the way down to the trash barrel. I should've given him a hug. Told him not to worry. Made him think everything would turn out okay. Only it was too hot. I'd do it later, if I remembered. At the moment, I had to get ready for evening customers.

None ever came, though.

That's the way it was a lot of nights. Days, too. Nobody stopped by The Diner. The item in the newspaper that'd tempted Cash to buy it in the first place made it all sound different: *"Ideal com'r'cl locat'n,"* it read. *"Sml. dwn. pymt. Lvg. qtrs. incl. Est. income, $300/mo."* Even Rosanne had been thrilled.

8

It turned out that "lvg. qtrs. incl." meant three tiny rooms tacked absentmindedly onto the back of The Diner, and lots of times we had trouble paying the gas bill, let alone raking in "$300/mo." The whole idea of The Diner was to give us something reliable to lean on until Cash found himself a really fast horse, one he could haul around to the big county fairs, even the state fair. A horse who'd win all the time, instead of just once in a while.

The whole business drove Rosanne crackers. "Day after day, we wait," she told me. "For customers or fast horses, whichever comes first. Meantime, Babe, my life is just drifting by. My figure slips south while I try to keep it hoisted north. It all makes me crazy, Babe."

When it got to be six o'clock, I knew there wasn't going to be any supper trade for sure. We eat early in my part of the country. Those who'd planned to do so at The Diner would've started arriving by four-thirty to eyeball our menu.

I washed the counter again, filled the sugar bowls and salt shakers, hung a new flystrip by the door, turned the dogeared card in the window so it read "Closed."

Cash would be home soon—if he hadn't stopped in Libertyville to drink some beer with his friends, that is. They were something else Rosanne didn't like: Cash's rowdy friends. But Cash himself was not a man to get mean and nasty after he drank a little beer. He just got mellower and more agreeable until finally he rolled off into a corner some place and fell asleep. It was the truth, though, that lots of times he didn't show up at home until two or three in the morning.

It would've been nice if he'd come home early for a change, would've made me feel like I wasn't so old and

9

alone after all. I wondered if Rosanne had left him a note. I went to check the pillows on their bed. That's the place people usually leave farewell notes—pinned right to the middle of their pillows. I'd watched enough TV to know that.

Only there weren't any farewell messages on either Cash's or Rosanne's. Then, as I walked out of the room, I saw she'd left him one in red lipstick on the mirror:

"Cash: I'm leaving. For good. I'm not coming back. Ever."

It had finally happened. The thing I'd worried about for so long. I felt colicky all of a sudden, like I'd swallowed big gulps of air. None of what'd gone on the whole afternoon was make-believe. A blue truck was not going to wheel back into our yard. Rosanne was not going to jump out of it, crying she'd almost made a terrible mistake.

My mother, Rosanne Carmody, had deserted us. She was not coming back to Money Creek. Ever.

Chapter 2

CHLOE BEGAN to cry again and held her arms up to me. Chloe was two and a half, but she didn't talk yet. "I don't believe that child has both her oars in the water," Uncle Waldo told us when she was two. "No such thing," I said. "Chloe is thinking. When Chloe gets done thinking, she'll tell us what's been on her mind. Her oars are just as good as anybody's."

A mosquito had bit her near the left eye, which was now swelled mostly shut. I hoisted her onto my hip, where her wet diaper quickly soaked me to the skin. Since Chloe felt disinclined to speak to us, trying to potty-train her had turned into a real adventure.

Quick as I could, I started to think about the Money Creek mare. That's what I always did when I got a colicky, heartsore feeling: *Think quick of something nice, Ella Rae*, I'd tell myself, *something to put starch back in your shorts*. It was testimony to the bad times we'd been having lately that we hadn't even named that red mare yet, in spite of the fact she was by far the prettiest piece of horseflesh Cash'd ever dragged home.

Now if you've never seen a bloodbay horse, you don't know what beautiful is. Cash always said, "There ain't no color that looks bad on a fast horse," but in my opinion some colors are certainly prettier than others.

11

Bloodbay is darker than your ordinary bay color, which is really just plain old brown. Bloodbay is not brown; on the other hand it isn't black, either. It's something in between, with a generous fistful of ginger-red thrown in to give it spice. When the Money Creek mare stands in the sun in the paddock Cash built for her across the road from The Diner, why, the way she looks is enough to send shivers up my spine.

"What'd you have to pay for that horse?" Rosanne wanted to know the minute Cash unloaded the red mare. There were rusty razor blades in my mother's voice. It was always Rosanne's way to speak harshly to my daddy; it was rare for anyone to hear him lay the same on her. But Cash laughed, pleased to seem thrifty for a change. "Didn't give hardly a nickle for her," he said.

That afternoon, as he faced us across the fence, his eyes so smiley and blue, his hair crinkly and blacker than a magpie's wing, I marveled at how I loved him. Later, I wondered why Rosanne ran off to California to ogle movie stars when she had one ready-made right in her own backyard. Buster and Chloe were lucky: they looked like Cash, with their blue eyes and midnight curls. I looked like Rosanne's sister Beatrice, who next to me was the plainest-looking girl I'd ever laid eyes on.

"You won that horse in a card game, right?" Rosanne grated. "You promised me you wouldn't play cards anymore, Cash."

"I know I did, Rosanne. And I won't, not anymore. I won't have to, see?" He smiled again, too happy not to tell her all about it. "I had to get into that game for a couple hands, Rosanne, after this little red mare got thrown into the pot as collateral. I knew it'd be the only chance I'd ever have to lay hold of a piece of horseflesh like her."

12

"So. Is she fast then?" Rosanne wanted to know.

"Fast? Well, no. Not exactly."

"Not exactly! Cash, for god's sake!" I can't say if Rosanne was truly religious or not, but she sure had a knack for calling on the lord over the least little thing. "If you aim to be in the horse-racing business, Cash, the idea is to be looking for the fast ones. Right? Who'd put a slow nag on the track on purpose?"

"I don't aim to run her, Rosanne. See, this mare's gonna be the foundation of our brood stock."

"Brood stock? She sure don't look like any brood mare I ever saw," Rosanne complained. "Why, she can't be more'n a two-year-old. I doubt she's ever been bred. So how can you tell what sort of colts she'll throw?"

"Just wait'll you take a gander at this little gal's papers, Rosanne, and you'll never wonder again. Why, she counts Man o' War himself among her ancestors. Not to mention Four Square and Challenger and Wishful Thinking. I aim to have this filly bred to Dark Victory up at Fairfield Farms—and the colt she'll drop us will put all of 'em to shame."

Sooner or later, talk about fast horses always ended up at Fairfield Farms. I knew it was a name Cash heard in his dreams. Fairfield Farms was located two miles outside of the village of Money Creek, on its own private, winding road. I'd never been there, of course; common folk did not venture up there uninvited. But people in the horseracing business came from all over the fifty states to breed their mares to Dark Victory or to buy one of his colts. Someday, I knew, Cash dreamed of naming his own place Money Creek Farms and fancied it might even rival that other place up the road.

We all walked to the fence beyond which the young

13

mare stood knee-deep in sweet clover. The sun on her coat made it shine until I thought my heart would bust. I had a failing, you see, for all those dreams of Cash's.

Cash emptied a cup of oats into his hat, held it by the brim, shook it. The whispery sound inside brought the red mare straight to his side. And right then and there it was plain to see why he never aimed to put her out on any race track. . . .

That mare's gait was the strangest, haltingest thing I'd ever seen. She seemed pigeon-toed to start with, and there appeared to be something terribly out of whack with her whole front end, like a car that's been rolled in a barrow pit and never been put back together right.

"My stars," Rosanne groaned, "that mare can hardly walk, Cash, let alone run. What's wrong with her?"

"Nothing that's going to keep her from making us fine, fast colts, Rosanne. She was caught in a pile-up on the track a few months back. Lots of horses went end-over-teakettle, so I hear. This mare ended up on the bottom. Her owners hung onto her awhile, hoping she'd get better. Decided it was hopeless, planned to put a bullet through her head. Only Johnny Esposito came along and bought her for a song."

If Rosanne doubted Cash's story he hardly noticed, for he was so thrilled by it himself. "Now you know as well as I do, Rosanne, that little Johnny E. knows horseflesh better'n anybody in these parts." Johnny E. sometimes rode Cash's horses in the Labor Day races at Chilhowee. "What Johnny don't know, though, is a good poker hand from a bad one. When I heard he was gonna put this mare in the pot in a game in Libertyville, I knew it was a chance that'd never come my way again. And you won't be sorry, Rosanne. No, ma'am, you'll never be sorry."

14

That was a month ago. Now we had a broken-down red filly, a diner where nobody dined, and Rosanne had taken herself a hike to California. And as the sun got lower, I realized it was another of those nights when my father, Cash Carmody, would not be home early.

"Hey, Buster!" I called. "C'mon, I'll help you and Chloe take your baths."

Buster began to cry again, too. There were mosquito bites all up and down his arms. "I'll sprinkle you some baking soda in the bath water," I told him, "and it'll fix those bites up so they don't hardly itch at all."

He grabbed onto my free hand. It was that melancholy hour of the evening that worried Buster, even during the best of times. He wanted to make peace. "I don't hate you no more, Ella Rae," he said. The way his life had been going lately, I knew he wanted to say something to guarantee I'd still be around when he woke up in the morning. "I know you don't, Buster," I said, and gave his hand a squeeze right back.

After he and Chloe had soaked in their soda-water bath, I dried them off, put clean underwear on them, and stashed them in bed. Chloe stuck her thumb in her mouth, and Buster was asleep almost before his head hit his pillow.

Then I got some sugar cubes from The Diner and went over to the paddock to call the red mare to the fence.

Cash's mudrunners were in the big pasture behind The Diner, but the mare seemed to enjoy her solitude. Cash allowed to me that he wouldn't ever put her out with the others, either, on account of her fragile condition. The moon rose behind her, poised a moment on the tips of her ears, vaulted into the darkening Missouri sky. I held out the sugar cubes in my palm.

"You're going to have to be named," I told her. "We can't go on forever calling you the Money Creek mare." Especially since I remembered too well that Rosanne insisted on calling the place Nowhere, U.S.A.

The air had begun to cool. The moon rose higher. A light wind came up and swept the mosquitos before it. In a ditch beyond the paddock, some fireflies lit their lanterns. Someone down the road must've cut a field of clover, for its bruised sweetness filled the air. Summer. In spite of everything that'd been going on, it was still my favorite time of year.

Summer . . .

"Come here, Summer," I invited, and jingled the cubes in my palm. She was named. No aggravation about it at all. With her around, not to be a common mudrunner, but to throw us colts who'd trace their lines all the way back to Man o' War, why, my summers might never end.

After I climbed into my bed in the room I shared with Buster and Chloe, I stared at the ceiling and waited for the sound of Cash's truck in the driveway. It didn't come till way toward morning.

I brushed my fingers under my nose; the smell of Summer was on them. A good smell. It was to me what the color red was for Rosanne. I thought about my mother and the growing experiences she was having in that blue truck loaded with chickens. I wondered how life for us Carmodys would ever get back to normal . . . whatever that was.

I was almost asleep before I remembered I hadn't hugged Buster and told him things would be all right.

Chapter 3

IF THE SLOPE of his shoulders next morning told how Cash felt about Rosanne's departure, I guess I'd say it was pretty bad. It was already hot by the time he rolled out of bed, and his night had been short, seeing he hadn't crawled between his sheets until three o'clock in the morning. But in spite of the summer heat, he held his hands around his coffee cup and hunched over it like he was chilled to the bone and needed warming up.

"She might be back quicker'n you think, Cash," I volunteered when I poured him a refill.

"Ella Rae, I don't understand how she could do it. I knew she wasn't always happy . . . but I never thought it'd come to this." His voice trailed off, thin and cranky as a child's.

"Whoa, Cash," I said. "Maybe it's a phase. Maybe teenagers aren't the only ones to have 'em. You can't tell—maybe she's on her way back right now. Maybe she decided she didn't want to go to California after all." Such words—even if I didn't believe them myself—I hoped would cheer him up.

He shook his head. "It'd be a pleasure, Ella Rae, it really would, to believe what you say. Only I got a hunch things are just as bad as they look."

17

"Thing to do, Cash, is keep your mind off Rosanne for the time being," I said.

"How'm I to do that, Ella Rae? She run out on me. Us, I mean. Only thing she left me was a message in red lipstick to be read at three o'clock in the morning."

To've read that message at three o'clock had been a matter of his own choosing. I saw no sense in pressing that fact on him. "You been talking about having that new mare bred to Dark Victory," I reminded him. "Means arrangements got to be made and all that. Maybe this'd be a dandy day to start 'em."

He brightened considerably. "You're a good girl, Ella Rae," he said. "You got a strong character, just like your Granmaw Carmody, you know that? You're right, too; I'll run up to Fairfield Farms soon's I shave and have a bite to eat."

My Granmaw Carmody had also been the person to tell me all about my immortal soul. "It's the only one you got, girl," she used to say. "It's more precious than gold and silver and diamonds all put together. Don't ever sell your soul, Ella Rae; it's worth more than anyone can ever pay you."

Cash washed and shaved and by the time he was done, most of the red had bleached out of his blue eyes. I fixed some toast and scrambled two eggs. He sat in a booth in The Diner under the red-and-white-checkered curtains I'd made in Home Ec class when everyone else was sewing on aprons. He washed everything down with a third cup of coffee. Then he was up and out the door, into his truck, and headed east toward Fairfield Farms. I didn't guess it then, but he was the only customer I'd have all morning long.

I knew arrangements like the ones he was going to make would take a while, so I was surprised to have

18

him show up less than an hour later, his shoulders slantier than they must've been when he first read his lipstick farewell. "What's wrong, Cash?" I asked. "You look like the dog just died. Weren't those folks at home up there?"

"Oh my, yes, Ella Rae. They were home, all right. I almost wish they hadn't been, though. If a person don't get bad news, he can pretend it don't exist."

"Can't be no news worse than what you got last night."

"Ella Rae, I know you got a talent for looking on the bright side. You say maybe your mama is on her way home, which don't seem likely to me. But on top of her leaving, what I heard this morning paints me a very deep, dark, black picture of our future. Do you know what those folks up at Fairfield Farms want as a stud fee for that Dark Victory?"

"How much?"

"Three thousand dollars of how much, that's how much."

"Whew."

"You ain't just whistling Dixie, girl. *Three thousand dollars!* Why, for a man who hires out by the day, races his ponies on weekends, got three kids but no wife, and a diner that can't pay its own way, three thousand dollars is just the same as three million. But don't I just *hate* the notion of breeding that fine red mare to just any old come-down-the-road kind of stallion."

"She isn't the red mare anymore, Cash," I said. "I named her last night while I was waiting on you to come home. Named her Summer. On account of it's my favorite time of year."

But Cash was too miserable to listen. If I'd told him I'd named his mare Miss Mud Hen he wouldn't have

19

heard me. He moped around The Diner, went out to the paddock finally, stood outside the fence with his hands hooked in his hip pockets, studied that mare as if some bright solution to his troubles might pop into his head if he concentrated on her long enough.

At noon, I fixed a pair of grilled cheese sandwiches and a side order of fries for a man and his boy who were headed to the mouth of Money Creek to do a little fishing. They paid me, and I watched Cash climb back into his truck and head out for heavens knew where. When Cash didn't know what else to do, he moved around a lot. He was like a hound who'll try to outrun the rusty cans tied to his tail.

The mail came late that day, right after Buster and Chloe went down for their naps. Buster was glad it was his sixth summer—meant he'd be in first grade in the fall and would never have to take another nap in his life.

I thought Rosanne might've dropped us a card from St. Louis. No such luck. Instead, we got a bill from the bread man and another from the Coca-Cola Company. Both were two months overdue. Dire predictions about the future of our credit were printed in red letters on the face of each one. I set them aside on a stack of other bad news we'd collected from the milkman, the bank, and the electric company.

To pass the time until Buster and Chloe woke up, I turned to the pages of *The Money Creek News*.

On the front of it was a blurry picture of Mrs. Denis Puckett-Smythe, who, along with her husband, owned Fairfield Farms. Neither of them was a Missouri native. The year I was ten, they'd descended on Money Creek, bought acreage for a horse farm, trailered in a stallion named Dark Victory, built themselves a half-dozen barns and a fancy house.

Now I was informed that Mrs. Puckett-Smythe had just returned from New York, "having attended many important social and artistic events." I stuck my tongue out so far in her direction I tasted newsprint on the end of it.

I passed on to news that Ira Snepp, who was sixty-three and blind in his left eye, had won a second GoKart championship over in Libertyville. I went to school with Ira's grandson, Oat Snepp. Once Oat tried to kiss me in back of the gym door. "Gramp's a fool for speed," he liked to boast. "Just loves life in the fast lane."

I traveled on to the want ads and read one of them three times before I realized I might've stumbled onto a solution to Cash's problem.

> *Household help wanted. Female preferred.*
> *Must be legal age. Experience necessary.*
> *Contact: Mrs. Denis Puckett-Smythe,*
> *Fairfield Farms, Money Creek, MO.*

I turned back to the front page. Cash said the Puckett-Smythes had enough money to set fire to a wet mule. I'd never seen Mrs. Puckett-Smythe with my own eyes. Hardly anyone in Money Creek ever had. Groceries were delivered; she never shopped for her own. She went to New York—some claimed even to Paris and London—to buy her clothes. Her house at Fairfield Farms had been built to imitate what somebody called Country French architecture. I peered at the face in the photograph; it looked small and pinched to me. I couldn't

21

tell if its owner was pretty or plain, whether her hair was dark or light.

Experience necessary . . .

Well, I sure had plenty of that. I watched the cars stream past on the highway outside The Diner, hurrying like Rosanne to places more interesting. I could call Aunt Beatrice, ask her to tend Buster and Chloe for me while I applied for that job at Fairfield Farms. I could close The Diner temporarily, until school started again in the fall. With my first paycheck, I could pay off the bread man. After that, the Coca-Cola Company. And all the while, be close to a certain fine horse named Dark Victory.

"Aunt Bea?" I had to ring three times before I got her. Aunt Bea, who was two years younger than Rosanne, had married Waldo McFee, owner of the OK Hardware Store in Money Creek, and got herself the pretty name of Bea McFee. Uncle Waldo was serious, worked hard, had money in the bank. "Rosanne hadn't been so headstrong, she could've done just as well," I'd heard folks say. They said it real regular, in fact. I knew Cash'd come to believe hell was not a four-letter word but a five-letter one spelled W-a-l-d-o.

"Aunt Bea? It's me. Ella Rae. Say, can you hop over here a minute to watch Buster and Chloe for me? I got an errand to do up the road."

"Ella Rae, I'm smack in the middle of rolling up my hair. Can't it wait, sweetie?"

"No, ma'am, I don't believe it can. Buster and Chloe are still napping, though, so they won't give you fits at all."

"Can't your mama watch 'em for you, Ella Rae? You tell her for me to raise her nose up out of those movie magazines."

"Rosanne isn't here, Aunt Bea. She took off yesterday. Went out there to California, just like she always wanted."

The sound Aunt Bea made over the phone reminded me of the racket that watermelon made when Buster dropped it off Granmaw Carmody's second-story porch and it broke into seventy-eleven pieces. "Oh, no, sweetie, she didn't . . . did she?" Aunt Bea finally found breath enough to groan.

"Yes, ma'am, she surely did," I told her.

"All right, Ella Rae. I only got a couple more curls to roll up. Then I'll be right over."

While I waited, I went out to scratch around in the weeds behind the trash barrel where weeks ago I'd flung an old red bicycle. The ground around the barrel was dusted with coffee grounds and sparkled with broken glass. Buster's aim usually was not much better than his intentions.

I hauled the bicycle upright, pulled wild grapevines off its handlebars, plucked a surprised green garden snake out of its spokes. Being garaged in the weeds had not improved its condition. The front tire was still flat. I ran to the back porch of The Diner, grabbed a tire pump, and pushed new life into it.

As I did so, Oat Snepp flew past on his new orange ten-speed. "Where you going, Bones?" he called.

"Off to make some magic," I called back, not caring if he understood or not. He didn't, and rode on, shaking his head.

Aunt Bea's hair, which was straight and mouse-brown like mine, was tormented into tiny sausages when she arrived. She had tried to bandage them up with what looked to me like a piece of pink mosquito net.

She looked on, amazed, while I fastened an old towel

around the bicycle seat. I did not want my south end to be dirty by the time I arrived at Fairfield Farms. There was no need to give my new employers cause to think poor folk had poor ways.

Then I put on my white jeans, borrowed one of Cash's white shirts, and fastened my hair into a granny knot at the back of my neck.

"You sure got a mind of your own, Ella Rae," Aunt Bea murmured.

"Might as well have," I said. "Nobody else seemed to want it." I waved her good-bye and wheeled out of the yard.

Chapter 4

FAIRFIELD FARMS covered 360 acres of prime Missouri land. Its hills were soft and rolling, its fences painted white and sometimes hidden by masses of flowering pink dogwood. The stream called Money Creek, for which our whole town had been named, flowed right through one corner of the farm. Inside its fences, horses of many sizes, shapes, and colors, all of them fleet-looking, grazed amiably together. I figured the sign at the Y in the road was the same one Cash must've read earlier in the day:

Welcome to Fairfield Farms:
Home of Dark Victory
Sire of Kentucky Derby Winners
Star Wind, Thunder Prince, and Highboy

I pedaled slowly up a tranquil aisle between twin rows of oak and willow to where an enormous house sat in a square of weedless green lawn. I parked my bicycle and rang the bell. The house was stuccoed, vanilla in color, and I decided those Country French folk knew what they were up to, for it was lovely as a dream.

Deep inside the house chimes began to sound. Soon, somebody's light, firm footstep approached from the other side of the heavy wood door. It opened, and there she stood. Maybe she didn't tend to her own grocery shopping, but she could still open her own door. It was Herself, looking very thin and very rich.

Rich folk actually *do* look different from the ordinary kind. You'd think the rich sort would be the fancier of the two, but it's the other way around. Rosanne, for instance, could deck herself out in enough jewelry, hair combs, fake organdy flowers, beads, bangles, and baubles to scare dogs right off the street.

Mrs. Denis Puckett-Smythe's style, on the other hand, was plain and spelled m-o-n-e-y. There was a strand of what I knew must be real pearls at her throat. None of that dime store stuff for her. Her hair was neither long nor short and was a rich lady's no-color color. Her face wasn't really thin or pinched, either, like it'd seemed in the newspaper picture. Her skin was white and smooth as marble; she probably used those expensive creams and lotions that Rosanne used to sigh over and wished she could buy.

But it was Mrs. Puckett-Smythe's eyes that held me fast that afternoon: they were clear and blue (though not as blue as Cash's), and were filled with a look I knew quite well myself. She was lonesome.

"Yes," she breathed to me. "May I help you, please." It should've sounded like a question, but being accustomed to authority, she did not bother to tack a question mark to the end of it.

"Ma'am, I'm here about that job you advertised in *The Money Creek News*," I explained. "Household help, that's what you said you wanted. Female preferred. Well—here I am."

"Ah. Of course. Won't you come in, my dear." Still no question marks. "Follow me into the morning room and we can discuss the matter.'' Imagine. So rich they had rooms for different hours of the day. We had three down at The Diner for the whole twenty-four. Our quarters were so cramped Cash said you couldn't cuss a cat without getting hair in your mouth.

The room into which she led me was filled with plants and flowers and in the middle was a glass-topped iron table painted white. Around it were white iron chairs with chintz-covered seats. Mrs. Puckett-Smythe studied me as though she'd seen me somewhere before. I was sure she hadn't.

With a glow of recognition still lighting her blue eyes, Mrs. Puckett-Smythe motioned me to sit down and offered me a cup of tea. ''Oh, no thank you, ma'am,'' I said. ''It's getting close to the supper hour for me. Best I don't ruin a good appetite.''

She nodded, pleased. ''You sound like a very sensible young lady,'' she murmured. ''How old are you, Miss . . . ah . . .''

''Ella Rae, ma'am. I'm sixteen.''

It was a fib, the first of many I'd soon find myself telling. I wouldn't be sixteen until September, after school started. I delayed giving her my last name. No sense in sprinkling too many clues around. ''I've got lots of experience, too,'' I told her.

''Indeed.'' Her clear eyes never left my face. ''Then you've worked in other homes in the community.'' No question marks appeared on the horizon.

''No, ma'am. I work for my daddy. He owns The Diner. It's way over there the far side of Money Creek. At the junction just before you peel off to go up to St. Louis.''

''Ummmm. I don't believe we've ever stopped there.''

''No, ma'am, don't believe you have. I would've

27

remembered." I hoped Cash had not foolishly given his name, either, or wailed out loud over the high cost of stud fees, and so have drawn unusual attention to himself.

"Do you wear a uniform at the . . . The Diner, dear?"

"A uniform? Oh no, ma'am. Just jeans and a shirt. They're always clean, though. When I do the laundry I pour in some of that blue stuff they advertise on TV."

For some reason, she smiled. "I'm sure you do, dear. We'd expect you to wear a uniform here, however. A white one during the day, a black one if we entertain in the evening."

"Whatever you want me to wear is fine with me, ma'am." It was the truth; I didn't care a whit what sort of costume she wanted to clap me into. For at that moment, beyond the ruffle of chintz that framed her morning room windows, I spied the object of my mission at Fairfield Farms.

Seeing my stare, Mrs. Puckett-Smythe turned to look out the window with me. "Isn't he the most amazing animal?" she murmured. "I never quite get used to him myself. I am astonished every time I see him in motion." She bent a smiling gaze on me. "That's Dark Victory, you know. Perhaps you saw the sign in the driveway."

Now as far as I was concerned, Summer was beautiful just because she belonged to Cash, because he had such high hopes for her. But the horse outside Mrs. Puckett-Smythe's windows was something beyond beautiful.

Oh, he was a handsome, high-headed dandy! He was liver-colored and tall as a house and wore a perfect white teardrop between his blazing dark eyes. Haughty as any prince, he paced restlessly up and down the length of the small paddock to which he was confined. The muscles under his gleaming coat romped like puppies playing under a satin bedspread. He was like no horse I'd ever seen or expect to see again.

"Does your mother know you've applied to us for employment?" Mrs. Puckett-Smythe asked, jarring me back to real life.

"My mother isn't with us anymore," I said.

Mrs. Puckett-Smythe put a thin, white hand to her throat. The look she gave me made me think she knew as well as I did how it felt to lose something you love. "My dear, I am *so* sorry," she gasped. "I didn't mean to be so clumsy. . . . I would never have asked if I'd known. . . . Please, dear, accept my condolences. When did she . . . did your mother pass away?"

"Oh, she didn't, ma'am. She took off for California. Yesterday. In a blue truck loaded with chickens. She said she needed to grow and have experiences. Had her little alligator suitcase packed quicker'n you could burn a tick."

This news seemed to make Mrs. Puckett-Smythe feel even worse—she turned pale and wilted in her white iron chair. Her hand fluttered against her throat. "I arranged for Aunt Bea to mind Buster and Chloe when I take this job," I assured her, hoping it might help. It was a small fib: Aunt Bea had only agreed to watch them for the afternoon. But I was getting ahead of myself. "That is," I added, "if I get this job, Mrs. Puckett- . . ."

"Smythe," she finished weakly. I'd never known if the *y* was short or long. It was short, just like plain old Smith.

"It's like this, Mrs. Puckett-Smythe," I explained. "We still got a life to live, Cash and Chloe and Buster

29

and me. I aim to be as much help to my daddy as I can be. That's why I'm here today."

Mrs. Puckett-Smythe listened to me, as amazed as Aunt Bea had been a half-hour earlier. She recovered her broken composure slowly, one piece at a time. "My, you *are* an arresting girl, Ella Rae," she sighed at last.

That kind of rumor could ruin my career as household help even before it got off the ground. "Goodness, ma'am," I said quickly. "Someone has traded you the wrong information. I've never been arrested. Mr. Redpill, our principal, scolded me once for jaywalking—but that's the closest I ever been to trouble with the law."

"No matter, Ella Rae," she murmured. She smiled at me in a puzzled sort of way. But it was clear she had also taken quite a shine to me. "I think we'd love to have you help out at Fairfield Farms," she said softly. "You might add . . . add a great deal to our lives."

How could she guess it was my aim to subtract, not add? "I'll be here bright and early tomorrow morning," I promised. Aunt Bea would certainly be surprised. She figured she'd done me a favor to watch Buster and Chloe for a couple hours on a single afternoon. Now it looked like she'd be blessed with them the whole summer.

When we rose from the table, a huge Siamese cat leaped into my chair. He regarded me with a jealous, cross-eyed gaze. I held out my hand. "Nice kitty," I ventured. He hissed and quickly stitched three red threads across my knuckles.

"Shame on you, Pooki," Mrs. Puckett-Smythe scolded mildly, never taking her gaze from my face. Her expression was a bit like Rosanne's when she studied the pages of her movie magazines; I figured it had to do with wanting things that stayed just out of reach. And

30

who should recognize that look better than Ella Rae Carmody herself? Because while Mrs. Puckett-Smythe studied me, I pondered the beautiful horse outside her chintz-draped morning room windows.

How long would it take, I wondered, for me to figure out a way to steal him away some evening for a few moments of stolen romance with a certain red mare . . .?

Chapter 5

HOUSEHOLD HELP. What would it entail, I wondered. I would scrub toilets, no doubt. Do some sweeping and vacuuming. Dust. Empty trash, like I made Buster do at The Diner. It didn't matter, of course. No task would be too common for my consideration.

My real mission, after all, was grand. Felonious, too. After it'd been accomplished, I would be a criminal. Even if no one ever discovered what I'd done, *I* would know. I tried not to dwell overly long on that aspect of my presence at Fairfield Farms. I pushed Granmaw Carmody's advice way to the back of my mind. To worry at a time like this about my immortal soul would only confuse everything.

When I arrived at Fairfield Farms for my first day of employment, Mrs. Puckett-Smythe seemed enchanted to see me, as though she had not been quite sure I would show up.

"Gracious, Ella Rae," she said to me in her breathy way, "you look so radiant! So fresh! Just exactly how a young girl ought to look!"

My radiance was no accident—it'd been accomplished by the sweaty, two-mile bike ride from The Diner. How fresh it made me was something else.

"Come, dear," Mrs. Puckett-Smythe said. "I want

you to help me cut and arrange some flowers. Friends are coming this afternoon from St. Louis. I want the house to be a symphony of color when they arrive.'' She smoothed my hair away from my cheek and admired my left ear as if it were an interesting shell she'd discovered on a tropical beach.

"Do you want me to put on a uniform first?" I asked.

Her laugh was light and brittle as glass. "No, dear. Just come along with me. I'll show you what to do."

Her flowers grew in neatly groomed levels across the sloping backyard of her vanilla-colored house. Such blooms! Gladiola and iris and lilies of every hue. Violets and baby's breath and painted daisies grew there as well. Mrs. Puckett-Smythe carried a large, flat basket into which she put the cut blooms, along with ferns she said were for background foliage for her arrangements.

She considered each bloom carefully before cutting it—each had to be perfect, I could tell—and directed me to lay it in the basket for her. Then she discovered a pale blue creeping flower with heart-shaped leaves among all the others. "Ummm, what do you suppose this is?" she worried out loud to me.

"Why, ma'am, that's morning glory," I told her. "You better get rid of it quick, too—it'll spread faster'n gossip if you don't."

She smiled at me like I'd said something awfully clever. Her face had gotten softer since yesterday. The lonesome look in her clear blue eyes seemed to have faded a bit, too. It was an ideal time to pose a question to her that'd been on my mind since the afternoon before.

"Why was it you ever came to Money Creek, ma'am?" I asked. "I mean, you could've gone most anywhere in

33

the world you wanted. Some folks say they hate Money Creek, that it isn't more'n a wide spot in the road.'' I didn't mention which folks I had in mind.

Mrs. Puckett-Smythe laid her green-handled flower shears aside and put her gloved hands on her knees. She gazed into the summer distance. Fog, pale as smoke, rose above the trees that bordered Money Creek. ''Maybe that was exactly it, Ella Rae,'' she explained. ''You see, we *could* go anywhere. Do anything. Do nothing. Did those things, in fact. Only life always seemed a bit . . . empty.'' She paused but did not look my way. ''Of course, we had our horses. Our friends put their money in gold or paintings or jewelry. We owned race horses. Once, on our way to Louisville to the races, we chanced to pass through Money Creek. . . .''

She turned to me and her eyes were suddenly bright. Eager. Like Buster's when he wants real bad for you to understand something he's trying to tell you but he can't find the right words. '' 'This is the place I've been dreaming about, Denis!' I told my husband. 'I'd recognize it anywhere! Now we won't just race horses, Denis—we'll raise them, too.' ''

It was plain to me she got her ideas the same way I got mine—suddenly. Then she went on: ''The minute I saw Money Creek I knew it was a place we could watch our horses be born, grow up, become famous. For Denis and me, such horses would be rather like . . . like children.''

Her voice trailed off. It sounded like Rosanne's, full of wishes for something she hadn't caught hold of yet. She had pastures full of horses, a yard gone crazy with flowers, and a vanilla-colored house, but somehow they did not fill up her heart.

''Well,'' I told her matter-of-factly, ''I sure don't

plan to live anywhere except Money Creek. Us Carmodys go back a long way in this neck of the woods. Yes, ma'am, five generations back, that's how far. You know that cemetery on the hill, the one you pass on your way up here from town?'' She nodded, eyes eager. ''It's loaded with Carmodys,'' I said. ''Spread out, my kin are, like roots from a tree.''

Mrs. Puckett-Smythe smiled and her touch on my arm was shy. ''What an enchanting picture, Ella Rae!''

''Picture, ma'am?''

''Of your ancestors being spread out like roots from a tree. Roots. That's what I'd like to have, too. Maybe you are luckier than you realize, Ella Rae.'' What she said might've been true. Only I wondered if she knew you got roots by staying in one place a long time. You didn't get 'em by being in New York or Paris one day and someplace else the next.

At that moment, we both looked up to see a very tall, very lean man come round the corner of the house and stride toward us through the flowers. He wore a handsome mustache and was togged out in boots that fit his legs like glove leather. His riding trousers were gray and had a faint shine to them. His shirt matched and sported tiny pearl buttons. He wore a visored cap and carried a leather quirt, which he tapped impatiently against his thigh. Granmaw Carmody would've said he was all done up in brown rags—which was to say he looked mighty grand.

''Ah, Maree,'' he said, ''I thought I'd find you with your flowers.'' He regarded me with a slight frown. ''And who is *this* young lady?''

''This is my . . . our new girl, Denis. I told you about her last night, remember? She's from down the hill, from down in Money Creek.''

"Of course—Ella Mae, isn't that right?"

"Rae, sir," I corrected. "Ella Rae, sir." Once again, I was stingy as a miser with my last name.

"Rae, yes; sorry. I've never gotten used to the quaint fashion you Southern folk have of using your two names. Billy Joe. Jim Bob. Katie Sue. How long will you be with us, Ella Mae?"

"Rae, sir. Ella Rae. I guess I'll be here—"

Before I could finish, Mrs. Puckett-Smythe rushed in to explain for me: "Ella Rae will be here only for the summer, Denis. Only for the summer." She'd advertised for household help; now she seemed to be apologizing about it. Her voice was quick and guilty as she went on: "Ella Rae is sixteen, Denis, and will have to go back to school in the fall. She'll just be a bit of extra help while we entertain this summer." It seemed real important to guarantee I was not going to be a permanent fixture. It was okay with me; my real job at Fairfield Farms would surely be done by then.

A sudden commotion from the nearby paddock distracted all of us at the same time. Mr. Puckett-Smythe's frowny face lit up. "Ah, here comes Myers on Dark Victory!" he cried. "I told him this morning that the horse badly needed some hard exercise. My, what an animal! You certainly knew what you were doing when you picked him from all the others, Maree!" Mrs. Puckett-Smythe beamed, pleased to be held responsible for Dark Victory.

Grady Myers, I knew from Cash's table talk, was the Puckett-Smythes' head trainer. He was also in charge of the breeding programs at Fairfield Farms, which made him a man to reckon with. But like the Puckett-Smythes themselves, he was not a Missouri native and so was held suspect by all the rest of us. I'd seen him once before in Money Creek at Waldo McFee's hardware store. Myers was a runty, surly little man with mean eyes—but mounted on Dark Victory on a bright summer morning, he looked more than the master of any situation.

Dark Victory, who must've stood a full seventeen hands, looked all leg and neck to me. He knew he was grand, and carried his small head high in the air. His eyes glowed; his tail swept the ground; his breath left his barrel chest in great whooshes.

But just before he came abreast of us, Grady Myers turned the stallion and laid him out in a flat, hard run around the far side of the paddock. It should've looked like hard work, but Dark Victory simply lowered his small, neat head, stretched out his powerful neck, and flowed rather than galloped around the paddock.

"Marvelous beast, don't you think, Ella Rae?" Mr. Puckett-Smythe asked proudly. Then he shrugged. "Of course, I suppose a girl such as yourself is really not that much interested in horses."

"Hardly at all, sir," I agreed quickly. "The critters don't do that much for me."

"We had a gentleman at the farm recently," Mr. Puckett-Smythe confided, "just a day or so ago, as a matter of fact. He had a mare, said she was a fine young thing, and he wanted to breed her to Dark Victory. Seemed terribly taken aback when I told him the service fee was three thousand dollars." Mr. Puckett-Smythe gave me an indignant glance. "It isn't much, you know, to pay for a sire the likes of Dark Victory."

My heart jumped into my throat. "Local man, was he?" I murmured. I had to know if Cash had blabbed his name all over the place. It was important to keep clues to a minimum.

Mr. Puckett-Smythe shook his head. "He never stayed long enough to tell me his name. He drove a battered truck, though, that I'd recognize anywhere. He left quite despondent, poor devil. I assumed he had high hopes for a mating between Dark Victory and his mare. He said she was a pretty little thing with lines that went all the way back to Man o' War."

When Grady Myers came down the fence a second time, Mr. Puckett-Smythe motioned him over. Myers reined the stallion back, but the horse had too much energy simply to stand there, still. He danced about on all four feet, turning smartly this way and that, mouthed his bit, dampened us with spittle. He glowered at us with blazing, white-ringed eyes.

"He's in fine fettle, sir," Grady Myers announced. "Too bad the Renfews' mare had to cancel today."

This news agitated Mr. Puckett-Smythe, who rescued his frowny look from wherever he'd put it to rest. "What happened?" he asked. "I thought their mare was in season and due here today."

"Was indeed, sir, but the Renfews called—mare sprained an ankle as they were loading her for the trip. They didn't want to truck her all the way up here and risk damaging her leg further." As he spoke, I fancied Grady Myers studied me with a small, mean eye. "Haven't I seen the young lady somewhere before?" he asked.

Mr. and Mrs. Puckett-Smythe scissored me between a pair of curious glances. "At the OK Hardware Store, sir," I said brightly. I had been there to buy a new halter for Cash the day he brought Summer home.

"Our dog, Lutie, needed a new bed," I rattled on. "Was due to throw some pups, Lutie was. A fine, blue-tick hound, that Lutie. My daddy paid a regular fortune for her. Tells me she hunts coon better'n any hound he ever owned."

Lutie had wandered in off the highway one day, stayed with us long enough to drill that hole in the back screen door, and left as easy as she arrived. Cash, as far as I knew, hadn't been coon hunting since he was fourteen years old. But I surely did not aim to tell a soul I was in the OK Hardware Store to buy a halter for anybody's red mare.

At noontime, I served Mr. and Mrs. Puckett-Smythe lunch. It'd been prepared by Helga, the cook, a lady built like a brick wellhouse, whose accent was thick as a mustard plaster.

The meal wasn't much, in my opinion. Sure nothing I'd be caught serving at The Diner. It was a piece of salmon in clear jelly stuff, all decorated up with sliced cucumbers for scales and pimento-stuffed olives for eyes. No wonder Mrs. Puckett-Smythe looked so skinny and peaked. But both the Puckett-Smythes dove into their meal with delight and drank wine out of a bottle with a name I couldn't pronounce.

Helga told me my station was just inside the kitchen door. "Station?" I muttered. "Stations are for trains and buses."

"That iss your station," she hissed at me, and gave me a stool to camp on while I waited. "When their meal iss finished, you clear off the table. Then you serve dessert. It iss your job. And that iss your station."

"Okay, okay," I agreed to keep the peace. "No need to tie your tail in a knot over it." So it happened that I was in a perfect position to eavesdrop, though it would never have been my plan to do any such thing.

39

"Isn't Ella Rae a dear, Denis?" I heard Mrs. Puckett-Smythe sigh.

"Ella Rae?" Mr. Puckett-Smythe's voice was blank. He'd already forgotten me. "Oh, yes, she seems like a nice little thing. Not so taken with herself as girls her age often are. Remember the Bentons' child? What a horrible little monster."

"Ella Rae isn't like that at all, Denis. Ella Rae is so fresh. Radiant. Unspoiled, that's what Ella Rae is. It seems to me she's bright, has so much potential. Did you know her mother deserted her, Denis? How could she have?"

"Now, Maree, I hope you aren't beginning to think . . ."

Mr. Puckett-Smythe's voice was tender but filled with some sort of warning. I hazarded a glance around the corner. He sat with his back to me, but his wife was in full view. She'd cupped her chin in her palm. She studied the garden beyond the morning room window. When she turned to look her husband in the face, the glances they traded brought a small, sad smile to her lips. She moved her hand toward his across the glass-topped table.

"I know what you're trying to say, Denis," she murmured. The tips of their fingers touched. "But it won't be like those other times, I promise. Not like when I bought that villa in France. Or the time I tried to adopt that little boy in Italy. Not even like when I was so determined to own Dark Victory."

Mr. Puckett-Smythe covered his wife's thin white hand with his own. "I just don't want you to start dreaming dreams again that can't come true, Maree," he said gently. "I don't want things to go wrong again, see you disappointed one more time."

40

"Oh, this is different, Denis!" Her voice was bright with good intentions but her eyes got shiny as if she might be ready to cry. "Ella Rae is only household help, darling. Just for the summer . . ."

Summer . . . the very name, filled with wishes, that I'd given to Cash's bonny red mare.

After working only two weeks for the Puckett-Smythes, I managed to pay off the bread man—the whole $48.12, which included the tax. The Coca-Cola Company came next. But on the evening after I settled my first bill, Cash mentioned at supper that Summer was in heat. She was ready to be mated. I knew my life of crime was about to commence.

Just the same, even with all that on my mind, I wondered what'd ever happened to the villa in France, or to the little boy in Italy who'd almost been adopted by Mrs. Puckett-Smythe.

Chapter 6

"IS THIS HERE caper you've invited me on liable to get me snuffed?" Buster asked.

"*Snuffed?* What sort of chin music are you playing me, Buster? That kind of talk makes me think you spend too many afternoons watching 'Perry Mason' reruns."

Buster peered at me through the gray haze of his glasses. "A child my age don't deserve to die or get thrown in jail," he observed piously.

"You aren't going to die or get thrown in jail either," I said. "What we are doing is not a crime. What we are doing is . . . is borrowing."

"If it was honest borrowing, Ella Rae, we would not need to be doing it at midnight."

"Hush," I said. That kind of reasoning had no place in my plans. Besides, it *was* borrowing. I aimed to pay back every penny of that $3,000 stud fee. I would work it off, as household help, for the Puckett-Smythes. I would have to work after school and weekends for years. They would say: "Here is your check for the week, Ella Rae," but I would press it back into their hands, fold their fingers over it, and shake my head. "Why, no need! Just to be here at Fairfield Farms is enough. Really! It's a pleasure just to be around you

42

folks. It's an opportunity might never come my way again.''

Buster and I kept to the far side of the road, our movement hidden in the fitful patterns of light and dark cast by the rows of oak and willow. The road itself, which wound between those rows, was a white ribbon in the starlight. The moon had not yet risen. I carried a flashlight and a stout length of rope that I'd borrowed for my mission from the back of Cash's truck. Buster toted some oats in an old bread sack.

I also had a map of the barn. Even though I was pretty sure I had our route memorized, I checked it twice, crouched low over it while Buster held the flashlight and I shielded its glare with my cupped hands. I stopped looking only when I was sure our route was burned into my brain.

"You think that horse'll ride us double going home?" Buster asked. "I'm tired already, Ella Rae, and we ain't even captured him yet."

"I doubt seriously if either you or me is going to climb on board Dark Victory, Buster. He's tall as some buildings I've seen and besides, he isn't your ordinary, everyday-type saddle horse. As for capturing—there isn't any to be done. That's the handy part. Dark Victory is just waiting in his stall for us to come and fetch him to Summer's side.''

Buster's words did give me pause, though. Time itself was a factor I hadn't exactly come to terms with. We had to get Dark Victory away from Fairfield Farms, down to make a colt with Summer, and back into his stall in barn number five—all by the time the sun came up. It was bound to be a squeaky schedule.

Dark Victory's barn, which housed other horses, too, was lit when we sneaked onto the grounds of Fairfield

Farms. "There's somebody in there," Buster announced. "Probably waiting for us with a shotgun." He turned on his heel, relieved as could be. "Might as well we head right on home, Ella Rae. We can't steal that horse tonight."

I retrieved him with a finger hooked in his collar. "No such thing, Buster. You scare too easy. They keep a light on at either end of that barn the whole night long. Sort of like that nightlight you had when you were four, remember?"

Two forty-watt bulbs burned at either end of the long center aisle of barn number five, but each stall itself was dark. The whole place smelled sweetly of fresh-cut clover hay and warm horseflesh. Dark Victory was at the far end, the end that was conveniently farthest from the big house. Buster and I padded along as silently as we could, our passage marked only by an occasional surprised nicker from the darkness of a stall.

Stall number twenty was larger by far than any of the others, Dark Victory having earned luxury quarters for himself with his record of begetting fleet-footed Derby-winning foals. The stall was locked, of course. Mr. Puckett-Smythe kept the master key in his office. One afternoon, when I was dusting, I made an impression of it in a piece of jelly wax I'd carried from The Diner. The key itself I made on a press down at Waldo McFee's hardware store one afternoon. I told him it was for my bicycle lock.

I opened the top half of the door. Dark Victory didn't come forward right away, so I stuck my head in. He came at me with such a rush I jumped backward and knocked Buster right to his knees.

"Ella Rae," he sniffled, "I think this scheme is starting off the way most of yours do."

44

Now Dark Victory might've been a proud, high-headed dandy, but he wasn't really mean. Just full of vinegar and honey, a horse with so much raw energy he seemed to light up the air around him. He rolled his eyes at me and whinnied—a booming, trumpeting sound designed to wake all my Carmody kinfolk down in the Money Creek cemetery. What was worse, he might wake everyone in the big house.

"Hey, fella, take it easy," I whispered. He wore a halter, as he always did, and I reached up to grab its ring. I snapped my length of rope to it. I opened the lower half of the door of stall number twenty. Dark Victory came through the opening like somebody'd set fire to his tail.

Poor Buster backed himself into a corner and held up his hands to make a prayer. "Rattle those oats in that sack," I told him.

"I can't, Ella Rae," he whined. "I'm too scared even to spit."

"Buster, you're about as much good to me as a side saddle is to a pig. Rattle those oats and worry about spitting later on."

But at the sound of the oats in that bag, Dark Victory sort of lowered his head like a bull and made a dash for Buster, his ears tipped forward like a pair of quotation marks. Buster leaped aside, dropped the sack, and took off down the aisle like it was now *his* tail that was on fire. I leaned over, scooped a few oats into my palm, and held them out to Dark Victory.

It occurred to me, a little late, that I might lose my hand right up to my watch band. But the stallion only lipped up the oats, lathered my hand with spittle, and breathed warmly in my face. "Okay, guy," I said, "how do you feel about a trip in search of some midnight romance?"

The idea seemed to suit him fine, and we started down the aisle to where Buster cowered like a ninny. "Open that door, Buster," I directed, "for we are on our way. Mission Impossible has almost been accomplished." I checked my watch. It was 1:30 A.M. We didn't have a minute to waste.

It might've been the starlight, or the crushed-clover smell on the air, or maybe the fact Dark Victory hadn't kept his date with the Renfews' mare. Whatever it was, he began to act crazy the minute we hit the outdoors. He lifted his head on that powerful neck, raised his nose to the stars, let loose a bellow that shook the ground under my feet. He began to dance around me like a savage around some tied-to-the-stake victim in a late-night movie.

"Ella Rae," Buster complained out of the darkness, "I see lights going on all over that big house." I snatched a look over my shoulder—sure enough, the place blazed like a Christmas tree.

I hauled down on Dark Victory's lead rope and tried to engineer him back into the barn. Still trumpeting like a fool, he followed me. I led him into his stall, unsnapped my rope, closed the door both top and bottom, and locked it. Buster stayed outside the whole time. He was taking no chances of being accidentally snuffed. I nipped out of the barn to join him, catching as I did so a glimpse of Mr. Puckett-Smythe and Grady Myers coming down the aisle from the opposite end.

I pressed my back against the barn door, let my breath out in careful gasps. From the other side I heard Grady Myers say: "I think someone's been trying to run a whizzer on you, Mr. Puckett-Smythe."

46

"I thought so, too," came Mr. Puckett-Smythe's voice, "when I heard Dark Victory set up such a commotion. But look—his stall is safely locked. Nothing really seems to be amiss at all."

Grady Myers was not so easily satisfied. "What's this, sir?" he exclaimed. "Looks like a bread sack. With oats in it. Mighty strange, I'd say."

Buster let out a groan and I had to clap a hand over his mouth to keep him from making a full confession then and there.

"We had some ladies touring the farm today," Mr. Puckett-Smythe mused. "Daughters of the American Revolution, I think they were. Maybe one of them . . ."

". . . carried a sackful of oats out here with her?" Grady Myers finished for him. "Well, sir, if you don't mind me saying so, I don't think it's too likely." Mean-eyed old Grady Myers. He'd ruin things yet.

But when I heard Mr. Puckett-Smythe answer, there was a shrug in his voice. "Who knows, Grady? Things seem to be all right now. I don't think we've got anything to be concerned about—at least, not tonight."

Their footsteps receded from us down the aisle. A door slammed. Buster and I crept for the fence, climbed over it, sank gratefully into the night-filled grass on the other side.

"One thing you can count on for sure, Ella Rae," Buster said.

"What's that?"

"If you got any other plans in your head, you just better count on carrying 'em out by yourself. I came as close tonight to ending up in jail as I aim to get."

The moon had risen, and by its light I could see Buster had firmed his jaw and made up his mind to take a whupping from me if that's what I decided to give him. "You can commit your own doggone crimes from now on, Ella Rae. I ain't going to be your a compass anymore."

"Accomplice, you mean."

"No, ma'am," he said. "Not that either."

Chapter 7

THE TIME during which Summer could be bred to Dark Victory would last only a few days. If she were not mated now, I would have to wait at least another four weeks until she came in season again. But if romance came her way right now, it would mean her colt would be born in eleven months—334 days if it was a stud foal, 332 for a filly—or about the middle of June. It was the perfect time for the birth of a first foal.

The matter was cinched in my mind—I would have to make another trip up the white road to Fairfield Farms. Two things would be different: one, Buster would not be my companion; two, Summer would. Taking her to him made a whole lot more sense anyhow.

As soon as I was sure Cash was asleep, and after Buster and Chloe had cranked up their little snore machines, I got out of bed, stuffed the map of the barn in my pocket, and slipped out the back door of The Diner. I put a bridle on Summer, led her out of the paddock, and was on my way.

I was starting at a later hour than my previous trip the night before and the moon was already on the rise. The night around us was filled with insect talk, and I had time to give Summer a lecture.

"Miss Moberly says the whole thing is natural. Natural, that's what you got to remember, Summer. The birds do it, bees do it, and horses do it, too." I sighed; it seemed a person could get her whole life in order and then things happened to upset it all. Like sex. "Dark Victory will know what to do even if you don't. Let's face it, Summer—since you are too busted up to ever show your stuff out on a racetrack, making colts will be your job. And the colt you'll make with Dark Victory is sure to be the fleetest thing between here and Pimlico."

Only what if she got shy, ran for the fence, tried to heave herself over it? Ramona Tilford, back in the eighth grade, had such a fit when Snooker Giles laid a hand on her knee that she threw up all over her pink dress. She claimed later it was all the Pepsi she'd drunk that did it, not Snooker's fat hand. Even after that dress was dry-cleaned it was still no good to Ramona. Even the Goodwill wouldn't take it.

Or what if Summer tried to outrun Dark Victory, fell, broke a leg? We'd have to shoot her. At least nobody had to shoot Ramona Tilford. No, no; I would not think of such disastrous possibilities! I would be positive, have starch in my shorts, just like always.

All day long I had listened in the Puckett-Smythe household for a chance remark about last night's excitement in barn number five. Nary a word was said within my range. Instead, I'd helped Mrs. Puckett-Smythe catalog her bookshelves. She said doing things like that with me were such a pleasure, and beat a fond look on me as we dusted and sorted books of all shapes and sizes. I was glad, though, not to have to look old Grady Myers in the eye. I had a feeling he would have been able to snatch the truth right out from where I'd hidden it.

I opened the paddock gate over which Buster and I

had vaulted not twenty-four hours earlier. I held my breath and listened hard. All I could hear was Summer's deep heartbeat. The lights in the barn were on. I slipped the bridle off Summer's head and turned her loose.

I sneaked into the barn, tried my key in Dark Victory's lock. I had wondered if they would change it. But no; my key still opened it.

Dark Victory, as though he'd been expecting me, stepped forward out of the darkness of his stall and obligingly lowered his head so that I could slip my rope onto his halter. He seemed as interested in my shenanigans as I was.

I knew the minute he smelled that red mare I might have a peck of trouble on my hands. I decided to release him into the paddock as quick as I could. I had not figured out exactly how I would catch him again. A bright notion might come to me later. I led him to the gate, through it, and set him free.

Summer looked up from her quiet browsing with mild surprise. I saw stars reflected in her eyes. Dark Victory circled her, danced about her, nuzzled her while she coyly dropped her glance. If she could've, that mare would've blushed. The stallion covered her neck with his, his dark mane tangling with her lighter one. She gave a soft cry of amazement.

Together, they began to move toward the dark arbor of wood that bordered Money Creek. I watched them go and got a pinched feeling in my chest. Long ago, had it been so soft and sweet and simple for Cash and Rosanne with their blanket of violets?

It was almost morning before the stallion came back with Summer. I had slumped down in the grass and dozed and woke to find them standing in front of me. I studied Summer. I hoped they hadn't frittered away their whole evening. It seemed to me she wore a smug look on her face. I decided it told me what I wanted to know. I slipped my bridle over her head.

But when I reached for Dark Victory's halter, he let me know he'd enjoyed the night air too much to go quietly back to bed. He raised his head and danced merrily away down the paddock fence. Oh, my god, I thought, calling on the lord just like Rosanne used to. "Come back here," I hissed. I chased him. He dodged me, stuck his heels into the air, told me he had no intention of doing anything of the kind.

A faint peachy glow now lightened the eastern horizon. I couldn't afford to get caught redhanded. I imagined the scene: Grady Myers would come down to tend Dark Victory in about an hour. He'd find the stallion loose in the paddock. There'd be no explanation of how he got there. On the other hand, there wouldn't be any trace that it was me who'd let him out of his stall. None. I'd left no footprints. I'd wiped the lock, left no fingerprints. Perry Mason used to dust for fingerprints; mine would not be found anywhere.

I led Summer away from Fairfield Farms, mounted her when we got far down the road. The stars had dimmed over my head; the moon was gone. No one stirred in Money Creek. I took to back streets like a spy. I yawned. It was going to be a long day, me having got practically no sleep for two nights in a row. I patted Summer's red mane; she flicked an ear at me. The air was a bit cool, so I put my right fist in the pocket of my jeans. My heart froze.

The map of barn number five was not there.

I laid awake a full five minutes the next morning before I remembered I was a criminal.

To know my life was changed forever made me feel weird. Now I truly did feel old. It might be a fact, as some folks claim, that crime doesn't pay. I also think it shortens your lifespan. At least, it was doing bad things to my heart, making it frantic as a trapped bird in my chest. And even though the morning was warm, my skin was clammy and cool.

I was so bewitched by my new criminal condition that I scarcely noticed the smell of coffee brewing. When I finally did, I thought: Why, it's downright decent of Cash to've gotten up early for a change and started it perking for me. . . .

Only it wasn't Cash who was making coffee in The Diner. It was a round, redheaded female I'd never laid eyes on before. She couldn't have been from around Money Creek. I knew practically every living soul within thirty miles each way.

"Who, pray tell, are you?" I asked. "And what exactly do you think you're doing in my diner?" She'd probably wandered in off the road like that little dog, Lutie. Maybe she'd been the victim of some prank played by a bunch of rude and rowdy friends. She'd be up and gone in no time. I decided to try to be polite.

Except she did not seem nearly as surprised to see me as I was to see her. "You must be the oldest one," she said, "the one with the strong character." She smiled amiably and showed me a dimple in her cheek and the sparkling gold corner of one front tooth. "Aren't you up early, hon? I thought girls your age generally liked to sleep the day away."

"I certainly am not like most girls my age," I told her crisply, "and I definitely am not in the habit of sleeping in. Especially since I have to run this diner single-handed. Ran it until lately, I mean. Its closing is

53

only temporary. I have to get up early to see that Buster and Chloe get over to Aunt Bea's. None of which explains *your* presence in *my* diner." I laid a hand on my hip and barricaded her only exit from the galley behind the counter.

Her mascara might've looked okay yesterday but now her eyelashes were clotted together in surprised little spikes that gave her whole face an astonished look. She studied me regretfully. "I came home last night with your daddy, hon. I guess you didn't hear us, it being so late and all. My name's Fronie. I'd like to be your . . . your friend." She held out a hand to me.

I stared at it like it was covered with warts. "Of course I didn't hear you," I snapped. *How could I have?* After all, I hadn't been in bed myself until nearly four A.M., thinking all the while Cash'd been sound asleep in his own. Only a night ago, Grady Myers had complained someone was trying to run a whizzer on Fairfield Farms. My punishment was that all the while, Cash had been running a terrible one on me.

I flew into his bedroom like an angel of vengeance. Took hold of one sun-browned arm looped over the bedside. Hauled him upright so quick I almost dislocated a shoulder. "Who's that female person out there?" I hollered in his ear. "You better have a doggone good explanation, Cash Carmody, of what she's doing in my diner."

He blinked like I'd brained him. "Ella Rae, your tone of voice surely does call up a memory of your mother. I swear both of you could put a firebell to shame."

"Don't natter on to me about firebells," I yipped. "I don't need lessons on how to brew a pot of coffee or stir up a mess of fries. Now you tell that woman out there to git. Pronto. You hear me, Cash Carmody?''

The ruckus I raised lifted Chloe and Buster right out of their beds. They stood in their underwear in the doorway of Cash's bedroom and pondered Fronie, who had followed me. Her robe—if you can call a garment as colorful as the ceremonial costume of some island princess a robe—caught Chloe's fancy. She sidled right up to Fronie and began trying to pluck off the exotic blossoms printed there on the fabric.

''Fronie's going to help us out for awhile,'' Cash told me. ''There's just too much for you to handle all alone, Ella Rae, what with the little ones and all, now that you're hiring out by the day just like me. We can bring Buster and Chloe home from Aunt Bea's, and maybe even open up The Diner again.''

''Cash, I got a feeling it isn't exactly my welfare or Buster's and Chloe's either that account for that woman being in this house. I don't know what you were thinking of, but Fronie was not what I had in mind when I told you not to dwell on Rosanne's leaving.''

I let go of his arm and he fell back against his pillows as sad and dashed as a wounded man. The look he gave me was the broody kind. ''Ella Rae, I don't believe your mama plans to come home. Ever. Not if what your Aunt Bea says is true. We are going to have to think about making a new life, Ella Rae. Maybe Fronie is part of that life.''

''Aunt Bea's always been confused. You've said so yourself.'' He used to say it lots of times. Maybe it was because of my big night at Fairfield Farms, but suddenly I felt tired as I could be. It was getting to be such a lot of work—trying to keep the tribe together, worrying over bills, hiring out to the Puckett-Smythes—plus pursuing a life of crime on the side.

I marched to the washer without a word and tossed in my white jeans and the white shirt I'd borrowed from Cash's side of the closet. Everything had to be spotless, for I was due back at Fairfield Farms in an hour. I poured in some of the blue stuff they advertised on TV. Why had Mrs. Puckett-Smythe smiled when I told her I used it? She ought to've known that a sixteen-year-old person (well, I was, almost), who'd practically raised a family all by herself would understand all about such things.

I didn't speak to a soul at The Diner for the rest of the week. At Fairfield Farms, I scrubbed all the bathrooms—there were four—spent hours dusting all Mrs. Puckett-Smythe's collectibles and replacing them in their glass cases, and vacuumed all the upstairs hallways.

"My goodness, you work so *hard!*" Mrs. Puckett-Smythe sighed in dismay. "Come—help me with my Japanese flower arrangements. I never intended that you should work yourself into such a frenzy!" With such a pretty garden, and being able to have bouquets of any size, she just the same fancied itsy-bitsy arrangements with a single flower leaning out slantywise and looking mournful.

When I got paid on Friday, I was able to settle up with the Coca-Cola man. The main thing on my mind was to figure out a way to get rid of that redhaired Fronie. The puzzle of the missing map vanished from my thoughts.

Chapter 8

BUT FRONIE was not a girl to pick up on a hint real quick. Finally I had to get downright mean. Nasty. Spiteful. When she made grits or fries for us, I allowed to her they were either too soupy or too greasy. I criticized her bookkeeping—since, with her help, we had reopened The Diner, and bookkeeping was once again important.

"Lordy, girl," I'd say, "who in the world ever taught you how to add and subtract?" I took aim on how she scrubbed the counter. "Got to watch those fingermarks, Fronie," I'd sniff. "Fingermarks all over the counter look so tacky." I speculated out loud on her taste in clothes. "My gracious, Fronie, at whose fire sale did you rescue that little gem?"

But about the worst thing Fronie ever said to me was, "Ella Rae, I declare you could stand some meat on those bones. Appears to me your belly keeps awful close company with your back bone." Well. What could you expect from a woman who looked like an unmade feather bed?

Of course, Fronie didn't have to give me a dose of my own medicine. If we were waging war—and we were, Fronie and me—she had all the equipment and most of the artillery because right from that first day,

Buster and Chloe were on her side. I couldn't believe it. If Fronie sat down anywhere, Chloe was sure to crawl right into her lap and lay there as contented as a cat full of cream. Buster was worse—he acted like a person in love.

Things got to be a whole lot worse when Fronie fetched her guitar from out of Cash's truck. It was a blue thing, with a riverboat scene painted on its face in Day-Glo colors. Its curved edges were sparkly with sequins. She would strum out a tune like "I've Been Lookin' for Love in All the Wrong Places," with the sort of enthusiasm that made me think she had. At such times, a look would cross Chloe's face that would make you think that fool woman had invented music all by herself. All the while, of course, Buster would hang onto Fronie's shoulder, the better to admire her dimple and her gold tooth.

Common little traitors, that's all they were.

Cash wasn't any better. He started coming home right after work nearly every night. He hardly ever stopped in Libertyville to drink beer anymore. Once, I picked up the phone in The Diner to find one of his rowdy friends on the other end. "What's happened to Cash?" he hollered in my ear. "Did he die or something?"

"Might as well have," I yelled right back. "I think he's taken up a new hobby."

There'd been many a time when I longed to have Cash come home early, to spend time with all of us, to be the one who'd mend the hole in the screen instead of me, to go with Rosanne to Parents' Night at school. Now he was—only I knew it wasn't because of any of us. It was on account of Fronie. I kept hoping she'd turn out to be just like that little dog, Lutie. That she'd wander off the place just as easy as she wandered onto it. Only she didn't budge.

"I think you're jealous," Buster told me. I stared at him like he'd slapped me on the cheek. It seemed to me his eyes were as little and mean as Grady Myers'.

"You're crazier'n Snooker Giles' pet coon!" I yelled. "Me? Jealous? Why, I don't even know how to spell the word."

"You like to run things," Buster insisted. "You like to be the one to make coffee. Now Fronie does. She sings, too. You can't sing a note."

"Believe me, I'd learn if I thought it'd do any good."

"Fronie says she's sort of a sub-stee-toot mother."

"Substitute? Why, that woman couldn't substitute for a monkey, let alone a mother. Much less Rosanne. But you're the one surprises me, Buster. You got a mighty short memory is all I can say. You cried your fool eyes out the day Rosanne left. You aren't any more faithful than Cash."

At which point Buster began to cry again. "She . . . Fronie . . ." He began to hiccup so I could hardly understand him. "She . . . she's soft and . . . squeeshy . . . and don't ever read movie magazines. She . . . t-t-t-ells me and Chloe a s-s-s-story most every night."

Soon after, Fronie took it into her head to have a woman-to-girl talk. Now look: I'd been old way too long to be talked down to by any redhaired woman who crawled into our house through a hole in the screen door.

"Ella Rae, hon, you and me might just well try to come to terms," she told me. "We don't need to hate each other like a pair of cats." Her eyes, which were brown, considered me with hope.

"Kindly do not refer to me as a cat, Fronie. I am just

59

trying to hold this tribe together until Rosanne gets back. And she'll be back, don't you doubt it for a minute. Probably on her way home right now."

"I doubt if that's the way it's going to be, hon. Not if what Waldo McFee tells me is true."

"Waldo McFee? You don't even know Waldo McFee."

"I met him just yesterday. Had to go down to buy a new fuse for the water heater."

"Waldo McFee," I insisted, "doesn't know anything except how to sell tenpenny nails or Elmer's Glue All at the OK Hardware Store. He couldn't have told you a thing that matters."

"Hon, it's like this: people change. Even mothers and fathers. What suits a person at sixteen don't always suit a person at thirty. I know, Ella Rae—I'm thirty, same's Rosanne. And I think . . . I think your mama has found a new life for herself."

"A new life? Just what's that supposed to mean?"

"Well, hon, lots of times it means a new fella."

"Rosanne hasn't found a new fella. She's maybe got a job out there in California, but you know well as I do she's still married to Cash."

"Oh, hon," Fronie sighed, "I think I know how you feel. . . ."

"No, you don't," I yelled. "You don't know and neither does Cash or Aunt Bea or Waldo McFee. I been doing everything I can think of and some I shouldn't have to keep this band of Carmodys together. To see Cash gets a chance to have a place called Money Creek Farms. All the rest of you just dawdle and diddle around like none of it mattered at all."

"Sure it matters, hon." Her voice was soft.

"Please do not refer to me as 'hon.' " She was the only one who ever had, though.

"Ella Rae, it'd be easier if we could be friends. Especially for your daddy."

"Why should he care?"

"He feels poorly that you are always in such a temper. Only thing that makes it bearable, he says, is you're up there at that big house most of the time."

"Well, maybe I just oughta stay up there permanently," I snapped. I didn't mean a single word of that, of course. I'd have just as soon gone someplace warm to shovel coal for all eternity. The Diner, with its chipped counter, plastic stool covers, and red-and-white curtains I'd made myself, was the only place in the world I ever wanted to be.

Little did I guess my time there was about to come to an end.

Wouldn't you just know it'd have to be mean-eyed old Grady Myers who'd find that map I'd made of barn number five?

Only it was Mr. Puckett-Smythe himself who laid its discovery on me. In the middle of the morning, he asked me to accompany him to barn number three, the foaling barn, where the night before one of Dark Victory's progeny had been born. Mrs. Puckett-Smythe was happy to excuse both of us; she said it gave her a chance to go over the week's menu with Helga. I never saw such a fuss over menus. What to eat occupied a lot of Mrs. Puckett-Smythe's attention, although she had no more meat on her bones than I did.

When we arrived at the barn and had clucked over the new colt—which was beautiful, with a blaze in his tiny face just like his daddy's—Mr. Puckett-Smythe held out his closed fist to me. I looked at it, puzzled. He opened it then to show me what was there. It was familiar: it was a tiny square of folded paper.

"What do you imagine this is, Ella Rae?" he asked.

I cleared my throat. "I believe, sir, when you open that up"—I coughed delicately into my own closed fist—"you will discover it is a map."

"Quite right, Ella Rae. Not only is it a map, it is a map of barn number five. Correct?"

"Correct, sir."

He unfolded the tiny square. "I might possibly not have recognized your handwriting, Ella Rae—but what was on the back of the map was a dead giveaway." He turned it over. How could I have been so dimwitted? I'd drawn the map on the back of a receipt from The Diner. Its message was cheerful: "Thank you. We appreciate your patronage. May we serve you again soon? The Diner."

"Would you like to know where Grady Myers found this?" Mr. Puckett-Smythe inquired softly.

"Where in the world, sir?"

"Right over here." He pointed to the paddock fence. "It also looked as if someone might've lain down in the grass for a bit of a nap. I wonder why?"

"I really couldn't say, sir," I murmured, coughing into my fist.

"Look at me, Ella Rae." I looked. It was the polite thing to do. "You were the one who was trying to steal Dark Victory, weren't you?"

I was shocked. My mouth dropped open. There were limits to the sort of thievery I'd had in mind. I had never intended to steal a whole horse.

"No, sir," I protested warmly. "I did not ever try to steal Dark Victory. I know it looks pretty bad all right,

62

you finding him loose in the paddock when you knew very well Grady Myers had left him locked in his stall. But no, sir, I most certainly did not try to steal your stallion, fine animal though he may be."

"Then what in the world were you trying to do, Ella Rae? Did you simply want to ride him? You might've been killed, do you know that? A stallion can be an unruly, dangerous animal. Dark Victory is not by any means an ordinary saddle horse."

We might've gone on discussing Dark Victory's personality for most of the morning but sooner or later, I knew I'd have to tell Mr. Puckett-Smythe what I had really done. "I only stole Dark Victory temporarily, sir—just long enough for him to make a colt with my daddy's red mare."

"Your daddy's red mare . . ." A light began to rise in Mr. Puckett-Smythe's gray eyes. "Does your daddy by any chance drive a beat-up old truck?"

"Oh, it's not really so old, Mr. Puckett-Smythe. Cash is kind of hard on cars, is all. He has a knack of backing too close to things. Or taking a corner too neat. Especially after he's spent a little while in Libertyville and is late getting home."

"Ah. It *was* your father, wasn't it, who came to Fairfield Farms several weeks ago to inquire about stud fees?"

"Yep."

"Ella Rae, do you realize the crime you have committed is called grand larceny in the state of Missouri? That such a crime is punishable by confinement in the state prison for up to twenty years?"

Just like Buster, wasn't he? Didn't pussyfoot around with bad news. My future stretched ahead of me: I'd be thirty-five years old before I ever saw Buster and Chloe

63

again. Buster would be a grown man. Chloe would be married, no doubt, and have babies of her own.

I'd look her up soon's I got out; I'd be pale as a ghost. Folks always get a poor color from having spent so much time behind bars. Chloe wouldn't know me. She'd come to her door, peer through the screen at me, latch it quick before I had a chance to step inside.

"Jeb," she'd call out to her husband, who'd be blond and come to the door with one of their children riding his hip, "there's a strange-looking old woman out here on our porch. I think you'd better call the sheriff on her. . . ."

The sheriff would turn out to be Oat Snepp. "Why, mercy, Bones, where in the world you been all these years?" he'd cry. Such was what my life had boiled down to.

"Why'd you do it, Ella Rae?" Mr. Puckett-Smythe wanted to know. I looked up, caught off guard by the blue note in his voice. "Maree . . . my wife . . . she tried to do so much for you. Paid you so well. Wanted to help you. I think she . . . we both . . . might even have begun to love you, Ella Rae."

I could've told him plenty about love. It's pretty hard to understand sometimes, for instance, and never quite what you think it ought to be.

"Well, sir," I tried to explain, my own voice now a trifle blue, "maybe it's like my Granmaw Carmody used to say: money will buy you a good dog but it won't make her wag her tail." We studied each other silently. He deserved a better explanation than that, so I gave him the real one.

"I did it for my daddy, Mr. Puckett-Smythe," I said. "See, Cash Carmody has come to think of himself as the sort of man who can't feed hay to a nightmare. I

64

don't fancy him feeling that way. He wanted so much to have that red mare bred to a good stallion. So I stole Dark Victory's services. And I know what it is, sir— just plain, old-fashioned stealing. Yes, sir, I know it, and I'm ready to pay my dues."

Mr. Puckett-Smythe never took his eyes off me the whole while I made my speech, only it seemed to me he heard something other than what I thought I said. When I was finished, he folded the map of barn number five back into its tiny square and slipped it back into his jacket pocket.

"You've been an exceptional daughter to Cash Carmody," he admitted. "Only I'm not sure he's been all that good a father for you, putting you in the position where you'd feel it necessary to steal for his welfare. Perhaps that is the real crime." He looked past me and paid great attention to the masses of flowering dogwood that bloomed against his paddock fences.

"For the moment, Ella Rae, I'd like you to keep this conversation to yourself. My wife and I will discuss what has happened and what should be done about it. But I want you to plan to have dinner with us tomorrow night. I think I might know a way out of this trouble that will be beneficial to all of us."

"No, sir, I won't say a word." I kept my vow, too. Didn't make a peep to Mrs. Puckett-Smythe or to Cash or Fronie either. *Grand larceny.* My stars, it hadn't felt all that grand. Oh, to see those two, that liver-colored stallion and our bonny red mare, pace toward the dark arbor of the woods that bordered Money Creek—that'd been grand, all right. As I watched them go, I hadn't really *felt* like a criminal.

I wondered if a colt begot by moonlight would be special, like hillfolk of the Ozarks exclaimed. More than likely, whether it was special or not, I would not be around to appreciate the fact. At least my new address would be easy for the family to remember: Ella Rae Carmody, c/o Missouri State Prison, Jefferson City, MO.

Chapter 9

WHEN I RETURNED that evening, the dining room at Fairfield Farms was mellow as a dream with its polished wood, candlelight, sparkle of silver, its crystal and lace. I was a guest, of course, which made everything prettier than ever.

When Mrs. Puckett-Smythe greeted me at the door, she did so fondly and touched the stray hairs that had escaped the granny knot I'd tried to capture them in. She smiled into my eyes with a bright eager gaze and held my arm as we walked to the dinner table.

Helga served us but managed to abuse me with her eyes the whole time. *"Thief!"* she sputtered in my ear when she set my pork chop in front of me. "I always knew you iss a thief!"

As pork chops go, it was a queer one, all decorated with orange sections placed like daisy petals in its middle. For folk who could afford any sort of rich food they wanted, the Puckett-Smythes sure favored a puny and peculiar kind.

Throughout our meal, which seemed endless to a person like me who awaited a sentencing, Mrs. Puckett-Smythe and her husband smothered me with smiles. We talked about the weather. "Just grand for June," was Mr. Puckett-Smythe's opinion. It was the evening that caught his wife's fancy: "I've never seen a prettier one." I offered my two cents' worth. "The moon will be full tonight," I said. Who should know better?—I'd watched it come up two nights in a row.

When we'd finished eating, we all went to sit in the living room, where Mr. Puckett-Smythe cranked up the air-conditioning so we could arrange ourselves in front of the fire he'd built.

"We want to talk to you about something very important, Ella Rae," Mrs. Puckett-Smythe began. "It might change the rest of your life."

"I reckon it's been changed a good deal already," I agreed. "Most of which I managed all by myself."

"Ella Rae," Mr. Puckett-Smythe went on (it seemed each of us would take a turn at speaking our piece), resting his elbows on his knees the better to lean toward me, "my wife and I think we know a way for you to cancel out your debt to Fairfield Farms. It all depends on your decision, of course."

"Well, sir, like I told you before, I'm ready to pay my dues," I said. "Just tell me what they are." Maybe they'd already decided on the same solution I'd had in the beginning: I'd work for them for free until that whole $3,000 was paid off. It'd take at least ten years. But that was only half as long as I might have to spend in prison.

Then it was Mrs. Puckett-Smythe's turn. "Ella Rae, you are too fine a girl, too fresh and radiant, and have too much potential to be living in the kind of circumstances in which you now find yourself."

I hadn't suspected I was as bad off as she made me sound. "We know it can't be easy," she pointed out, "to look after a younger brother and sister and try to get along with that new woman who is running The Diner

68

now." They already knew Fronie? Well, she was a girl to get around, sure enough. Look how chummy she got with Waldo McFee—enough to pry gossip about Rosanne out of him, at any rate.

But I couldn't let them believe their grievances were ones I had myself. "My stars," I told them, "it isn't as bad as you make it out to be. The Diner is a fine place to live. Really. You know those red and white curtains, the ones right there at the front windows? Made those myself. And Buster and Chloe?—why, they're hardly any trouble at all! Soon's we get Chloe potty-trained, life at The Diner will be practically perfect. Maybe Rosanne'll come home one of these days, too. You just never know."

"You're a brave girl, Ella Rae," Mr. Puckett-Smythe admitted. "You have a knack of looking life right in the eye."

But it was not my courage or eyesight that were on his wife's mind. "We want you to come to live with us at Fairfield Farms, Ella Rae," she blurted out. "We think we can do a great deal for you, prepare you for the sort of life you *really* deserve. And then all of us can forget about what happened between your father's red mare and Dark Victory."

"Live . . . *here*?" I echoed. I looked around the room like I'd never seen it before. Everything was so polished and lovely. The fire was fragrant and cheerful. Music filtered through the air to my ears. The carpet under my feet was something Mrs. Puckett-Smythe called Oriental. Pooki lay on his chair and considered me with a superior blue gaze. None of it was like The Diner, for sure.

"Oooohhh," I groaned, "I'm not sure I'd . . . fit in here."

Mrs. Puckett-Smythe closed her thin white hand over mine. "Don't answer tonight, my dear. We just want you to know we've both been waiting for someone like you for such a long, long time."

She said it so clearly, so simply I knew it had to be the truth. Only it's hard to be loved when you can't love back. Loving Cash, Chloe—even Buster—was no trick. I just did, that was all. But I was a different person now from the one I used to be. I was a criminal. I'd done that thing Granmaw Carmody warned me about. I'd sold my soul.

"Thank you, ma'am," I said. "For not wanting an answer right this minute, I mean. Maybe it's a good thing we all get to sleep on the notion. You might have second thoughts," I finished hopefully.

"Oh, no, Ella Rae," she assured me with a gentle smile. "We could be so wonderful for you. And you could be even more wonderful for us. I don't doubt it for a second."

I walked down the hill through the mild Missouri evening and marveled at how my life had gone to hell in a handcart. The whole summer had turned into a disaster: Rosanne had taken off, I was a thief, Cash had taken up with a redhaired woman. But one thing I was certain of—I could not go up to Fairfield Farms to live. I didn't care if they promised me Oriental carpets up to my kneecaps. I belonged with my tribe at The Diner. Even if that darn Fronie had to be included.

Except when I got home to The Diner, I discovered I didn't have a whole tribe anymore. Buster and Chloe had been kidnapped.

I was still a fair distance from The Diner when I saw someone stuffing Buster and Chloe into a dark blue car that had some sort of gold and silver insignia on its side. I gave a whoop and a holler and flew down the hill, but the car whirled out of the yard before I had any chance at all to demand an explanation.

Off down the road it spun, in the opposite direction from the one Rosanne's flight had taken her. Buster and Chloe knelt on the back seat, and their faces loomed at me through the window like a pair of small, round moons. Chloe had her thumb in her mouth. Buster's eyes were huge behind his glasses. He mouthed a plea to me: "Don't . . . let . . . them . . ."

I dashed into The Diner like a demented person. Fronie's face was all puffed up and red from crying and Cash held his head in his hands like it ached something terrible. "Someone's kidnapped the kids," I cried. "Did you get a good look at their faces, Cash? How much money did they want? We'll raise it somehow—"

"Ella Rae . . ."

"Fronie can get on the phone to the sheriff while we're gone. Waldo McFee can drum up a posse and . . ."

"Ella Rae," Cash groaned, "please don't invent more trouble than we already got."

"Don't just sit there," I shrieked, paying no attention to his words. "We got to hurry if we aim to rescue Buster and Chloe."

"We ain't going to rescue them, Ella Rae. It's the state that took 'em. Not even you can fight the whole state of Missouri, Ella Rae."

"What's the state of Missouri want with Buster and Chloe? I don't even have Chloe potty-trained yet."

"That woman who took 'em—said her name was Miss Rowe—said the kids weren't getting the proper raising."

"Proper raising?" I was astonished. "Why, I been

doing the best I can, Cash. You know that. They got bathed almost every night. Clean clothes three times a week. They looked okay to me. Sometimes Buster looks a trifle peaked, but you know yourself what a picky eater he is. Those dumb glasses don't help his appearance none, either, in my opinion."

"That social worker, that Miss Rowe, she said your Aunt Bea called her and said the atmosphere here was bad."

"What's wrong with the atmosphere? You mean on account of we don't have an air conditioner in The Diner? Well, we'll just get one. Charge it, like you did the TV. Fact is, I think Waldo McFee's got some on sale right now."

"It was the moral atmosphere that was bad, she said," he repeated.

"The moral atmosphere?" That could mean only one thing. I darted a fierce look in Fronie's direction. "See what you've gone and done?" I yelled. "You went and brought the kind of atmosphere in here that's caused us to lose Buster and Chloe. It's your fault, Fronie." At that, she squeezed her eyes shut and began to cry again, very softly.

But Cash would have none of that. "Now, Ella Rae, don't you hassle Fronie like that. Fronie didn't come here uninvited. I asked her. Furthermore, I want her to stay."

I couldn't believe what I was hearing. "You mean you'd let go of your own flesh and blood, your very own children, for . . . *her*?"

"Don't put words in my mouth, Ella Rae. I don't mean I aim to give up Buster and Chloe." He dropped his aching head into his hands again. His tan seemed to have faded considerably. "It's just that . . . well, there

72

are times, Ella Rae, when a man feels just about ready to give up."

I hated such words. If they'd been tin cans, I'd have kicked them all the way up the street. "Maybe I should sell The Diner," Cash mused, mostly to himself. "Go off somewhere new, you know, start fresh. I been waiting so long, oh so long, for a fast horse. Maybe it's time I put such notions aside. . . ."

As he spoke, something began slowly, slowly to leak out of me—like the air kept leaking out of that bicycle tire. My overdue bills were suddenly due: ones caused by Rosanne's leaving, by Chloe being so hard to potty-train, Aunt Bea turning traitor, that job at Fairfield Farms, which left me only a few hours each day to be with the family I loved. Not to mention the fact I'd made a criminal out of myself trying to give Cash something he wanted so bad.

"You don't need to move away, Cash," I said. "You and Fronie can have a new life right here. Without chick or child. And have your fast horse, too. See, I got Summer bred for you."

He raised his head to look at me. His blue eyes were red around the rims, this time not from a long night spent in Libertyville. "Would you kindly repeat that, Ella Rae? I've heard so much strange news lately I don't think I caught you right."

"You did, Cash. Summer's been bred. She'll drop you a colt next spring. About the twenty-second day of June, according to my calculations."

"Lord, girl, who's she bred to? Not some old worthless stallion you located in somebody's back pasture, I hope."

"I got more brains than that, Cash. She's bred to Dark Victory. Just like you always wanted."

73

"Dark Victory? Now, Ella Rae Carmody, don't you sit there and try to run a whizzer on me."

"No such thing. I took Summer up to Fairfield Farms two nights ago. She made a colt with Dark Victory. In the moonlight. Right down there where Money Creek runs through the stud farm."

"Ella Rae, we don't have three thousand dollars for a stud fee—as you surely ought to know. What you've done amounts to thievery."

"Worse than that. It's called grand larceny. I could be put in jail for twenty years."

"We'll have to get a lawyer. You're still a minor, so . . ."

"Don't worry, Cash. The Puckett-Smythes know all about it. They've agreed to forget the whole thing."

Cash's blue eyes narrowed. He hadn't heard so much bad news that he'd completely taken leave of his wits. "Why should they forget it, Ella Rae? They're in the horse-breeding business. They're not going to give away the services of a prize stallion because they like the color of your hair."

Fronie had stopped her infernal sniffling and her brown eyes darted from one of us to the other like she was a spectator at a Ping-Pong match.

"Actually, Cash, that's exactly what they aim to do," I said. Then I sighed. I was about to give him something he'd never had before: his freedom. Rosanne had started the ball rolling. Now I'd give it an extra shove. Cash was right: I couldn't fight the whole state of Missouri. Besides, I *was* a criminal. Talk about creating atmosphere.

"Starting tomorrow," I told him, "I am going to live with the Puckett-Smythes. Them and me, we made ourselves a bargain. They will forget what I did if I will live with them at Fairfield Farms."

At that, the last bit of color drained out of Cash's face. "Ella Rae, you belong here. You are . . . you are a Carmody." He reached for my hand, and I permitted him to squeeze its fingers. I didn't squeeze back. "You're my daughter," he said softly.

I didn't look at him. I couldn't. "Well, Cash, all the starch is gone out of this girl's shorts. Things have gotten into such a mess none of us will ever be able to straighten them out. This way, we can all start clean. You got Fronie. Buster and Chloe got the state. And the Puckett-Smythes got themselves something between a longed-for child and a filly with possibilities."

I marched into the room I shared with Buster and Chloe. Used to share. It had been the summer of our undoing. I was writing the final chapter myself. I stuffed my clothes in a paper sack. In eleven months, a colt would be born to Summer—only I wouldn't be around to celebrate its arrival.

75

Chapter 10

MAREE AND DENIS—that's what they asked to be called—
loved me in their fashion, and part of that fashion was
to change me as fast as possible into their dream child. I
had good basics, Maree assured me, which only needed
a little prodding here, a little polishing there, until I
would be exactly what they had in mind.

To start with, my hair was trimmed. Mrs. Puckett-
Smythe—Maree, I mean—was tickled with its color,
which I'd always detested as being dull, but which she
explained to me was unique. She showed me how to
pluck my eyebrows, too. Not too much, she cautioned,
for the natural look was in. Why, I'd been in fashion all
along and hadn't even known it, for hardly any girl I
knew was more natural than me.

Every morning after I took up residence at Fairfield
Farms, we went horseback riding. Sometimes it was the
three of us, sometimes just Maree and me. I was given
a dandy sorrel horse named Redbird to ride. It all meant
I had to have a riding outfit.

One wasn't enough, either. When we went to St.
Louis in the Puckett-Smythes' shiny black car, driven
by Grady Myers, Maree and Denis shopped at LaSalle's
Sporting Goods Emporium and I ended up with three
outfits. We also stopped by an art museum. In front of

it was a piece of metal sculpture called *Tormented Woman*. She did indeed look very uncomfortable. Maree told me that looking at such things would be part of my new life.

On the sly that afternoon, I bought a postcard at a drugstore. Buster, Cash'd told me on the phone the day before, had been taken as a foster child by the Branches, who lived just two doors from that traitor, Aunt Bea.

"Hi, Buster," I wrote. "I hope you're doing good and the Branches feed you stuff you like to eat. I will try to hop down and see you first chance I get. Hugs and kisses, E.R." I got a stamp out of a red, white, and blue machine with a little crank and dropped the card in the mail before the Puckett-Smythes noticed what I was up to.

Rosanne really liked to watch TV, but the Puckett-Smythes weren't into that at all. Instead, in the evening, we read to each other. At first, I figured it was a real dumb way to pass the time. All right for children, maybe, but for grownups? I was surprised how much I liked it.

"The world is mine: blue hill, still silver lake,
Broad field, bright flower, and the long white road;
A gateless garden, and an open path;
My feet to follow, and my heart to hold . . ."

Mrs. Puckett-Smythe would read in her high, sweet voice, her no-color hair as smooth as a bird's wing against her cheek.

"Those words belong to Edna St. Vincent Millay," she told me, eyes soft in the lamplight. It didn't seem to matter if the words she read were sad or glad: the

77

lonesome look was altogether gone from her eyes. I looked at Denis.

He was happy too.

One morning, Maree pierced my ears. She chilled them first with an ice cube and held a cork behind each one before running a needle through the lobe that Helga sterilized with alcohol. I was given real pearls to wear in them. Later, I got shirts and pants and nightgowns and such an assortment of clothes as I would never be able to wear out.

There were times at night, though, when I lay wide awake in the silky bed in the room the Puckett-Smythes said was mine, that I didn't feel like myself at all. I felt like somebody's invention. The Ella Rae Carmody I used to know had disappeared.

It wasn't long before she really did.

"Raella," Maree mused dreamily to me one morning at breakfast after I'd been with them for four weeks. "Isn't that a pretty name, dear? It has such . . . oh, I don't know, such a pretty sound!" She wrinkled her nose at me and touched my hand with one long, white finger.

"Yes, ma'am," I agreed, mainly to be pleasant. "Whose is it?"

"It's yours, dear. Your new name. Isn't that *exciting*? Ella Rae—only it's been turned around. The end first, the first the end. Raella. Oh, I do so like it!"

I cleared the frog out of my throat and tried to explain. "I'm named after Granmaw Carmody," I said. I had to hang onto at least that part of my history. "She's one of my kin who's spread out like a root from a tree on the cemetery hill. Remember? I told you about the cemetery hill. . . ."

"Yes, dear. I remember. It was such an attractive picture. But that's past, dear. We must think of the future now. The *new* you. Raella. Let's just say it is the name Denis and I have picked for you." She smoothed my hair, rubbed my cheek. I felt like one of the pieces of porcelain trapped behind the glass in the cabinets in her living room—something to be set in place, admired, dusted off now and then.

Maree winked saucily at me. "My name isn't really Maree, you know," she confided. "Well, it is and it isn't. Once it was spelled Mary. Plain and ordinary. So I named myself something prettier." She had a regular passion, I could see, for making things into what they weren't really.

Straight off, she ordered sheets and pillow cases with my new name embroidered on the hems. I also got monogrammed towels to hang in my own bathroom. The four of us had shared a bath at The Diner. It hadn't seemed so bad. An *R* by itself looked a lot different from an *ER*, too. I doubted that I'd ever get used to it, the way Maree hoped. It was one of those things that can happen to a person who's sold her soul.

About getting used to things—neither Pooki or Helga ever got used to *me*. They weren't about to, either, no matter what I was called. Pooki managed to snag my ankle every time I passed up the stairs on my way to my room. Helga never missed a chance to hiss "Thief!" in my ear.

The Renfews' mare finally was able to keep her date with Dark Victory, and on the afternoon when Denis helped Grady Myers load her for the journey back to her owners, Maree asked me to read an article in one of her ladies' magazines.

Its title was "Famous Mothers and Daughters of the

South." It had lots of pictures of mothers and daughters with their arms looped around each other or gazing into each other's eyes. "I know the man who wrote that article," Maree mused. "I wish he'd known about you, so we two could have been in it. We'd have been so perfect!" I couldn't see how—we weren't mother and daughter. Every day that passed, Maree seemed to let that fact slip out of her mind.

She was right about one thing, though—I was slowly getting to be perfect. To *look* perfect, I mean. The person I saw every day in the mirror was one I hardly knew. Her hair was smooth and shiny as Maree's. Her eyebrows didn't look like caterpillars. Her clothes fit. Cash's baggy white shirts were a thing of the past.

But being perfect takes a lot of hard work, and I am glad I didn't bet good money that Maree was through changing me—because it turned out that my hair, the condition of my ear lobes, and my name were only the start. When the three of us were having lunch one day on the patio, Maree came to the table with a smile and a thin catalog.

"This is from Eustachia Hayden, an old and dear friend of mine," she beamed. "She's headmistress at the Hayden Institute—a sort of finishing school for young ladies in Louisville, Kentucky. I went to the Institute myself, Raella. Oh, it's just the most wonderful place—and I know you'll love it as much as I did."

My hands turned as cool and still on either side of my lunch plate as a pair of trout on ice. I studied her catalog politely. "Aren't I . . . finished enough yet?" I asked feebly. I looked to Denis for help. He beamed, too. The idea of me at finishing school seemed to suit him fine.

Once more, Maree smoothed my hair. She did the

same thing to Pooki every time she passed him. He enjoyed it more than I did. She smiled happily, proudly, into my eyes. I was pained to see how much store she set in me. "It will be marvelous for you to go to finishing school, Raella! You'll become everything you were meant to be."

I looked out over the lunch table. Dark Victory, proud and high-headed as ever, dashed up and down his paddock fence. I wondered how big the seed in Summer's belly had gotten. Did the foal she was making for Cash have tiny hooves the size of my little fingernail? I reflected on Buster and Chloe, adrift on an ill wind like dandelion fluff. I thought about myself, headed to Louisville, Kentucky, to get finished.

When I slid between my smooth, initialed sheets that night, I decided I was as finished as a person ever needs to be. I felt done for. Used up. Empty. To have ended up in prison might've been better. That sentence would've been over in twenty years. The one I'd agreed to take might last the rest of my life. It was an awesome thought.

I remembered the card I had mailed to Buster. Buster couldn't read a word. What was the matter with me? He wasn't even in first grade yet. And the only hugs and kisses I'd given him in a long time were the ones I'd put on paper. . . .

Before Denis and Maree drove me to St. Louis and stuck me on a Greyhound bus bound for Kentucky, I managed to sneak a call to Cash. Fronie answered the phone. "Where's Cash?" I asked.

"Why, he's gone to Blue Springs with Johnny E. to run some horses, hon. You want me to give him a message?"

"Tell him I'm leaving."

"Leaving? Where're you leaving to, hon?"

"Mars," I said, and hung up. Why should they care? They had each other.

The windows of the bus were tinted green and the inside of the place smelled like cleaning solvent. I felt colicky and heartsore again but couldn't find anything nice to think about that would put starch back in my shorts. My whole life long I'd sworn never to leave Money Creek. At least Rosanne had walked out of it by her own free will. I was being shipped out like some sort of package.

I worried about how I'd locate Mrs. Hayden's school. You could see from one end of Money Creek to the other; you didn't have to worry about finding anything. It was all out there in plain sight. I needn't have gotten myself in a stew: as soon as I got off the bus in Louisville, a man in a crisp blue uniform came up to me. I thought maybe he planned to arrest me, that the Puckett-Smythes had changed their minds about our deal.

"Miss Puckett-Smythe?" Blue Uniform inquired in a tone of voice that let me know I was not the sort of parcel he'd expected to collect. "Miss Puckett-Smythe?" he sniffed at me again.

"You're looking at her," I said. "Is that all you want to know?"

His nose was thin and pointed on the end and his eyes were set remarkably close to one another. "I've been sent to fetch you to the Hayden Institute for the Refinement of Young Ladies. My name is Beatty and I am the chauffeur for the Institute," he said through gritted teeth. "Please come with me, madam."

He took my elbow in his gloved palm. Before Rosanne

82

had left for California, she and I had watched a show on TV about a girl who got kidnapped in New York. The people who did the job looked perfectly respectable. One even pretended he was a policeman. Now that I was the child of rich folks, I had to be careful. Besides, I was in enough trouble—and far enough from home—without being snatched.

I jerked my elbow out of his grip.

"I'll thank you to keep your mitts to yourself, mister," I said loud enough for the whole bus station to hear. If he decided to snatch me anyhow, drag me off, stuff me into the trunk of his car, there'd be plenty of witnesses. Someone would have time to jot down the license number. A bulletin could be issued for my rescue practically before he pulled away from the curb.

Two amazed spots appeared on his cheeks. "Well—I never!" he huffed.

"You bet you never," I said. "I'll find my own way to the Institute, if it's all the same to you. I don't aim to get finished even before those folks have a chance to work on me."

Astonished glances followed us as we marched, side by side like two soldiers into battle, through the doors of the bus station—him to climb into what looked like the kind of car they use for presidents in parades, and me to hail a cab off the street. A cab might not've been safer, but I had the satisfaction of choosing it myself.

It was a surprised Mrs. Eustachia Hayden herself who welcomed me into a white-columned building that faced a quiet street across from a small park and which bore a plaque with a legend that read:

The Hayden Institute
for the Refinement
of Young Ladies
Established 1912

I would soon learn to call it the HIRYL, along with the rest of its inmates.

"My goodness, aren't we glad to see you!" Mrs. Hayden trilled when I told her who I was. She did not comment on the fact I'd arrived by cab. She clapped one of my hands between two of hers. She'd said "we." I peeked around her to see who was with her. I couldn't see a soul.

She steered me into her office, which was painted blue. It had blue carpet and was hung with blue drapes through which a weird blue light was cast across our faces, making both of us look like we needed to take some soda for our stomachs.

"Mrs. Puckett-Smythe—dear Maree—was one of our most outstanding graduates," Mrs. Hayden confided. "Maree has been a credit to the ideals we uphold at the Hayden Institute," she added and squeezed my shoulder like she'd known me a long time. "We are all so delighted she's found such a lovely daughter of her own. Why, I understand that adoption proceedings are already under way."

Adoption? That'd be lots worse than getting a bus ticket from Rosanne. I wanted to remind everyone who and what I really was: *My name is Ella Rae, and I'm a woods' colt.* Instead, I asked, "Ma'am, could I ask you a personal question?"

Like Maree Puckett-Smythe, Mrs. Hayden had nerves that were like a fiddle string drawn too tight, and my

84

request took her unaware. "Gracious, dear, ask me anything!" she said, her eyes dark and darty.

"How long will it take me to get finished?" I wondered. "I don't want to rush you or anything, but I'm anxious as I can be to get back to Money Creek and . . ."

Mrs. Hayden was relieved and made a pleased bow-knot out of her thin lips. "Why, aren't you the sweetest thing! To want to get home to Maree and Denis. It's plain you love them as much as they love you."

Not exactly, I thought. I was mad that day I hung up the phone on Fronie. But now, with so many miles between all of us, I had a feeling that all I needed was a little time to plan, to hatch an idea, and us Carmodys could get out of the mess we were in. . . .

"Back to your question, dear," Mrs. Hayden said. "How long does it take to get finished, as you so charmingly put it?" She lowered her voice and looked at me like we shared a secret. "We are never really finished, are we? We are always learning how to be a bit more polished, a bit more sophisticated. It is a task that is never really over for us."

I was sorry to hear it. I'd hoped that once I got to be one, a lady that is, that would be that. "You see, Raella, it is a changing world. Fashions and expectations and obligations change, too. We must be on our toes every minute of every day, mustn't we, to be successful women of society." She peered at me thoughtfully through the blue haze of her office. "Fortunately, you are already thin," she added.

To be thin clearly was a step in the right direction. If I ever got a chance, I'll tell Fronie that to have a belly that kept close company with your backbone was a big asset in some parts of the world. She'd never believe me, of course.

There were other things Mrs. Hayden wanted to know about me. "Stand up, dear," she directed briskly. "Stroll around the room a bit. Let me see what else we have to work with." She spoke as though I were a piece of machinery that might be found to want a little oil. A slight adjustment here. A tightening up there. I got up and did my imitation of a stroll. Ordinarily, I'd just have got right off that chair and walked across the room and been done with it.

Mrs. Hayden was crazy about my stroll.

She clapped her birdlike hands together. "Marvelous!" she breathed. "Maree was right—you do indeed have a certain natural, jungle grace, my dear. Why, we'll be able to train you to enter a room so that heads snap and jaws drop."

Jungle grace? Only a minute ago she'd been talking about getting finished, and how it'd take years and years, and how even then you'd never be sure you'd made the grade. Now we were into lions, leopards, and tigers. But I was stuck.

"Yes, ma'am," I sighed. "I'll do my level best to crack a neck or two."

She pinched my cheek with delight. Persons like me, who've sold their souls, discover they've forfeited any right to refuse to have their cheeks pinched.

Chapter 11

MY ROOMMATE at the HIRYL turned out to be a girl named Priscilla Witherspoon who came from Baltimore. She had been there most of the summer getting finished. Down the hall from us was a girl named Nancilee Adams from Atlanta, and her roommate was DeLoris Monroe from New Orleans. DeLoris was doomed, I could tell right away, to have trouble turning out the way Mrs. Hayden wanted, for she packed about twenty too many pounds around her southern hemisphere.

It might've been my jungle grace that did it, but most of those girls, except for Priscilla, did not seem to cotton to me right off. Or maybe it was because all the brown rags in the world couldn't hide who I really was—just plain, old Ella Rae Carmody from Money Creek, Missouri.

Though Nancilee Adams hailed from Atlanta, she toted no Southern accent around with her. I remarked on that fact in a voice I judged to be friendly, but she looked me up and down like I had a bad smell. "My diction," she informed me, "is the result of my extensive training in Shakespearean theater."

"No kidding?" I marveled. I would've liked to hear more about it, since the closest I'd ever got to Shakespeare was listening to some crummy jokes Oat Snepp told about Romeo and Juliet. Nancilee Adams was not in a mood to share much with me, though, and yawned in my face.

"And where do you come from?" she asked as if she already knew my answer would bore her to death.

"Money Creek, Missouri."

"What a perfectly dreadful-sounding place." She yawned again. "It must be positively minuscule. I've never even heard of it."

"You would've if you were a fancier of fast horses," I said. "We raise racehorses in my neck of the woods. They're second to none anywhere in the world."

"And I presume your father is a jockey." She said the word like some little kids say words they get their mouths washed out with soap for. Johnny Esposito's nose would've been put badly out of joint by the way she snickered behind her hand. I wanted to ask her how you have a horse race without jockeys. Then, following her lead like sheep over a cliff, a few of the other girls began to snicker, too.

"My daddy," I said, and nearly choked to attach the word to Denis Puckett-Smythe, "owns Dark Victory. Our stallion has sired the last two Kentucky Derby winners. Star Wind took on a field of five, had the lead by the half-mile pole, and finished in one minute fifty-eight seconds. The track was sloppy, too. It's a record that hasn't been broken yet."

"I somehow cannot imagine *you* being connected with any kind of winner, even one with four legs."

"Oh, we Carmodys like the life," I said airily, but her words hurt. Cash wanted so bad to lay hands on a real winner. Yet here I was, not even admitting I was his daughter. "Fairfield Farms is absolutely grand, even

88

if you never heard of it. Our house is just the color of vanilla pudding. Pretty as a dream.''

"I thought Mrs. Hayden said your name was Puckett-Smythe," Nancilee murmured, and peeked at me from beneath her lowered lashes. A sly look stole over her perfect little face. Her hair, which was smooth and hung to her waist, was the color of clover honey.

Lord, lord, what was happening to me? I couldn't keep my fibs straight anymore. "Oh, it is, it is!" I lied cheerfully. "I'm a Puckett-Smythe on one side and a Carmody on the other." In a weird way it was absolutely true.

"If the Puckett-Smythe side raises horses, what does the Carmody side do?" Nancilee purred, luring me down a liar's path.

"Oh, that part of the family is all taken up with the restaurant business. They make money hand over fist, seems like. You know that Colonel Sanders and his Kentucky Fried Chicken palaces? Well, that's the Carmody's line. Fry up frog legs, that's what. Hush puppies. Slabs of catfish, too. Make a mint doing it, don't you know?''

"No, I wouldn't know," Nancilee said. "Furthermore, I think you're a liar, Raella Whoever-You-Are. I can spot one a mile off.''

"Well, my daddy always said it takes one to know one," I chirped brightly. I didn't know what Denis Puckett-Smythe's opinion was, but it sure was Cash's favorite saying.

Nancilee was not used to having folks call her number. She gave me a long, evil, hexing look and I knew I'd made my second enemy at the HIRYL. (The first had been Beatty/Blue Uniform.)

But Nancilee was not through with me. "Obviously," she murmured, "your folks' money is new. New money is never as good as old money. Ours is old. Real old. We've been rich longer than any of us can remember."

"Honeybunch, as long as it's green and the bank likes the shade, I don't complain." This time it was my turn to crank giggles out of the girls. It was something I could see Nancilee Adams had made up her mind to get even with me for.

When we went to bed that night, Priscilla told me not to worry too much about it. "Nancilee has a knack for being hard on people, especially newcomers."

"I thought maybe you felt the same way," I told her. "I mean, it's plain as egg on your face I don't exactly come from the same walk of life as the rest of you."

"Our walk thinks pretty well of itself," Priscilla admitted with a wry smile. She seemed to want to talk more about it. "My father is almost as rich as Nancilee's. He's been married four times. I think he's got number five picked out—an exotic dancer this time. He gets older but his wives don't."

And I'd been worried because Cash might end up going around the track twice. An exotic dancer. Maybe she had a bathrobe like Fronie's. "Do you like her?" I asked. "I mean, the one who might be number five?"

Priscilla shrugged. "I don't think it'd matter if I do or not. Besides, by the time I get used to her, number six might be coming in the door."

"Must be awful hard to remember everybody's birthday," I said. "Or even whether or not you should send 'em a card. Pretty soon you'll have a whole book full of ex-mothers."

Priscilla looked at me. She was pretty but pale, and the melancholy look on her face sorta ruined her good looks. "I like you, Raella," she said. "You're . . . well, I don't know . . . kind of different."

"Folks frequently comment on that fact," I said.

My first full day at the HIRYL was spent learning how the place was run, where and when the meals were served: in the Great Hall at eight, noon, and five P.M., sharp—or you didn't get fed. Priscilla said her boarding school was run the same way. She said that was where she stayed when her father was on his honeymoons, which was a lot of the time. On the second day, after we'd tidied our rooms in the morning, we watched a deportment movie.

I thought deportment was when you got sent out of the country. I wondered where I'd end up. What if they sent me to Puerto Rico? I couldn't speak a word of Spanish. Buster wouldn't be able to write to me, even after he got into first grade, on account of he wouldn't be able to address his letters in anything but English. I wouldn't be able to send any card to him, either, because I wouldn't know a peso from a penny and might not be able to work the stamp machine in a foreign country.

I was lucky for a change. Deportment turned out to be learning all about how to conduct yourself. We watched a long film about ladies and girls getting up and sitting down. They crossed their ankles but never their knees. I got a horrible backache from sitting so long in one spot, paying attention. About eleven o'clock I began to feel awful thin and hungry. To help pass the time, I entertained myself by wondering what Summer

91

and Oat Snepp were doing in Money Creek at exactly the moment I thought of them from where I was at in Louisville.

Then Mrs. Hayden asked us to imitate what we'd seen on the screen.

Nancilee Adams got to go first. She walked across the room like she had a pain in her pelvis. I thought I knew how she felt. She sat down gracefully, though, and didn't make the mistake of crossing her knees. Priscilla did all right, too, but I felt a little bad for DeLoris. When you're carrying watermelons on your hips it complicates a lot of things.

When it came time for lunch, we were served something called spinach soup. What those people did to spinach ought've been against the law. Anyone with a lick of sense knows you are supposed to fix spinach like collard greens: boiled with a piece of fatback, a little water, let to cook down until you have a nice, thick pot liquor which you can pour over a biscuit or a piece of johnnycake. But no, those folks pulverized their spinach to death in a blender, poured cream over it, and then, for heaven's sake, sprinkled nutmeg on top of it. I ate mine because I was so hungry, but that surely was the only reason.

After lunch, Mrs. Hayden made an announcement. "This afternoon," she told us, "we will rehearse appropriate conduct for an intimate party in one's own home." I'd never gone to many parties, but when Granmaw Carmody was alive we went to her house a lot for supper.

"For such occasions," Mrs. Hayden went on, "it is perfectly permissible for even the most sophisticated hostess to serve her own guests." Well, Granmaw

Carmody had been right in style, bless her heart. "The high cost of servants these days may mean that such a sensible economy might provide a bonus elsewhere in one's budget," Mrs. Hayden reminded us. Maybe that was how Granmaw had been able to save up for that trip up to Chilhowee to see her sister Maudie the summer before she died.

On a pretty silver tray, Mrs. Hayden had arranged some little things called canapes. "The Duchess of Windsor herself used to serve at some of her own parties," she explained so that none of us would think twice about the risk we were about to take. The canapes were little circles or squares or diamond shapes cut out of a slice of white bread and spread with olives or cheese or tuna fish. You'd have to eat a heaping plateful to ever get full.

But in case you got real hungry and desperate, Mrs. Hayden had arranged some oysters on the half shell. She never told us what she did with the other half. Why anyone would take a notion to swallow an oyster raw was something else she didn't explain. The trick was to squeeze lemon juice over the poor thing, then down the hatch. I decided I'd pass.

Nancilee was the first to practice serving Mrs. Hayden, who was our pretend-party guest. Mrs. Hayden was wearing a nice blue dress. I remembered the drapes in her office. She really liked blue. Maybe she'd had the dress made out of the same piece of material. As I watched Nancilee, I decided that girl didn't really have joints in her knees. Or elbows either. They must've been made out of rubber. They bent so easy and never cracked once.

Then it was my turn.

I lowered the silver tray to the proper level so that Mrs. Hayden, who was perched on the sofa, could pretend to serve herself. I smiled like I was supposed to. The oysters were snuggled safely on their half shells. When I felt Nancilee's toe in front of my own, it was too late to stop what was doomed to happen.

She had inched her foot in front of mine like she'd had a lot of practice at such things, just enough to upset my balance. Then, almost like slow-motion, the tray in my hands tilted forward and downward at the same time. To have tried to catch those oysters as they flew off would've been like helping Buster and Chub Murphy catch minnows barehanded along the bottom of Money Creek.

The oysters flew off the tray like so many barn swallows in front of an autumn wind. They dashed through the air and three of them, as if bewitched, plunged down the front of Mrs. Hayden's blue drapery party dress.

"My goodness, Mrs. Hayden," I groaned. "Am I ever *sorry*! I don't know what happened. It seemed like . . ."

Maybe getting finished to perfection means being able to look just like Mrs. Hayden did as those three oysters slid one after the other down her bosom.

First, she looked surprised. Then came an expression that made you think she'd suddenly remembered an appointment she'd forgot to keep. She rose slowly and smoothly from the sofa. Her manner was so royal even the Duchess of Windsor would've been envious.

Mrs. Hayden moved gracefully from the room. None of us girls said a word. A stranger to the scene would never have guessed, either, the fight those three oysters

94

were probably having in the front of her dress. Mrs. Hayden was so cool about it all she didn't start to run until she hit the bottom of the stairs.

I was amazed when I started to laugh. But I felt a whole lot worse when I couldn't seem to stop.

Chapter 12

By MY SECOND week at the HIRYL I decided that Nancilee Adams, good friend though she might be of Shakespeare, had a heart as black as a tar ball. The Oyster Outrage was followed in short order by the Kitchen Crisis, thanks to Nancilee. She had to have laid awake half the night hatching such capers.

That's where I was when the ruckus started. In bed. After all, it was eleven-thirty at night.

"Everyone down to the Great Hall," I heard Mrs. Hayden call imperiously through the second-floor hallway. There was an urgent note in her voice. "Please, everyone, down to the Great Hall *immediately*!" I figured maybe the place had caught fire, so I hopped out of bed right away.

The Institute wasn't on fire but Mrs. Hayden, I was sorry to see, was in a state of considerable agitation. It was spelled out all across her forehead, in between the strips of Scotch tape that were glued there.

"They're for her wrinkles," Priscilla whispered. "It's a trick movie stars use. One of my daddy's wives—I think it was the third one—did it, too. You paste them on and leave them overnight and in the morning you're supposed to look ten years younger." I wondered if Rosanne had heard about it yet. It seemed like a clever idea and not too expensive, either. A whole roll of Scotch tape down at Waldo McFee's was only about ninety-eight cents and would be enough for lots of nights' worth of wrinkles.

"I have something to show you, girls," Mrs. Hayden informed us. Her voice was quivery with indignation. She waved us to follow her and we all marched toward the kitchen.

Which was a sight to behold.

Someone must've decided to have a party while the rest of us were getting ready for bed. Blue Uniform, maybe? The refrigerator door stood open. A carton of milk had been spilled inside it. Rings of mustard and pools of catsup covered the counter. Cookies had been dropped on the floor and mashed underfoot. Potato chips were everywhere. A head of lettuce had been torn apart and now its wilted leaves lay like limp green scarves over the edge of the work table.

I'd have been fit to be tied if I'd walked into The Diner and found it in such a mess.

It was clear Mrs. Hayden felt the same way about her kitchen and was having a hard time finding words to describe such feelings. "I want to know . . . which one of you . . . found it necessary to raid the kitchen . . . and make such a dreadful mess of everything." She began to wring her hands and their blue veins stood out starker than ever under the glare of the kitchen lights. Her face, except where it was held together with tape, was getting splotchier by the minute.

"No one," she gasped, "is going . . . to leave this room until I have the name of the girl who committed this havoc in the kitchen of the Hayden Institute. Not if it takes the rest of the night."

The floor under my feet was cold. Each of us girls

studied one another with suspicion. Or I thought we did. I wondered myself what sort of person would make such a mess in someone else's house. Mrs. Hayden was dead right; it'd been a spiteful thing to do.

Nancilee stood opposite me and concentrated on her toes. I paid careful attention to mine. I stifled a yawn. I hoped someone would confess pretty soon. Nancilee cleared her throat. She looked at me full in the face with the sweetest, saddest little smile. She began to chew daintily on her lower lip as if the decision she'd just reached had been a painful one.

"I didn't want to be the one to tell you, Mrs. Hayden," she sighed, "but . . . well, it was Raella, Mrs. Hayden."

Mrs. Hayden's jaw didn't drop to her collarbone one bit faster than mine did. "*Raella?*" she echoed. "Maree Puckett-Smythe's own Raella?" She stared at me in disbelief. I looked back at her, just as astonished. When that little Lutie dog came to us she'd been full of ticks. Cash picked them off of her, one by one, then told me to soak a rag in turpentine and disinfect each place she'd been bit. Turpentine on a raw sore can burn like fire, and the minute we turned that Lutie loose, she rolled herself, hollering and howling, into the dust. That's just how Nancilee's words made me feel: like I wanted to roll on the ground, and holler and howl.

Instead, I heard myself stammer: "I n-n-never intended t-t-t-to . . . that is . . . maybe I got some sort of fever and didn't realize . . ." *You're a liar, Raella Whoever-You-Are*, Nancilee had said. Had I got so in the habit of telling fibs and lies that I was going crazy, too?

"I don't understand," Mrs. Hayden wailed, and I thought she might be getting ready to cry. "Maree and

Denis Puckett-Smythe will be so humiliated. I don't know how I'll tell them that . . ."

"Maybe you don't need to tell them," I suggested helpfully.

Mrs. Hayden screwed me into the tiles on the kitchen wall with an outraged glance. "We will discuss *that* later, young lady," she snapped. "Right now, you can fetch a bucket from underneath the sink and get a brush and some soap and commence to undo the damage you have done here tonight."

So, at midnight, I found myself scrubbing the kitchen at the Hayden Institute for the Refinement of Young Ladies. Mrs. Hayden shooed the other girls back upstairs to bed and watched me like a hawk as I washed and polished and put things back in order. The longer she watched me, though, the more perplexed she looked.

"You scrub like a person who really knows how," she observed. That fact caught her by surprise—after all, scrubbing was not a skill they taught at the Institute. I decided maybe it'd be a dandy time to confess about my Past Life: how once I ran a diner singlehanded, once had almost potty-trained a two-year-old female child, once had stolen a mate for my daddy's fine red mare.

But before I said a word I darted a peek at Mrs. Hayden. Her thin brows were drawn into a disappointed frown. With a clawlike finger she picked mournfully at the Scotch tape pasted on her forehead. I ran my tongue over my teeth but otherwise kept it still. On second thought, maybe it wasn't the right moment to be talking about anybody's past life, let alone one that belonged to a person called Ella Rae Carmody.

"Raella," Mrs. Hayden sighed when I was finished at last. "You truly don't seem to be the sort of girl who would . . . I mean, Maree Puckett-Smythe wouldn't have chosen you in the first place if . . . and you know, since the Institute was established in 1912, we've never turned out a failure. Never."

"I'm sorry, ma'am," I said. "I seem to be causing a lot of that lately."

When I got back upstairs—it must've been at least two or three o'clock in the morning, that same strange hour Cash used to sometimes come home from Liberty-ville—the halls of the HIRYL were empty. The lights weren't very bright, and it reminded me of the aisle in barn number five. It made me realize that whoever instigated the Kitchen Crisis was no worse a criminal than I was myself. When I passed the door to Nancilee's room, I heard a riot of giggling from the other side. Not that I was surprised.

I crawled back into bed and Priscilla's voice, small and thin in the dark, came to me: "You okay, Raella? I wanted to help you scrub, but I knew Mrs. Hayden wouldn't let me."

"Hey, don't worry about it," I said. "Everything's cleaned up slick as a whistle. It wasn't the death of me. Or Mrs. Hayden, either." Just the same, I was glad she'd wanted to help me out.

The next day, before lunch, I slipped out of the HIRYL and hiked down the street two blocks. I'd seen a small grocery store there the day I arrived by cab. I went in and bought a large jar of the cheapest peanut butter I could find. If I'd been buying it for The Diner, I would've got the best. For my present purposes, I wanted the kind that'd been extended with plenty of cottonseed oil. When I got back to the room I shared with Priscilla, I turned the lid just enough to break the seal, and set the jar on the window sill in the full glare of the sun.

"I don't believe I'd do that if I were you," Priscilla

advised. "Why, in no time at all, Raella, that peanut butter will be rancid as can be and you won't be able to use it for anything. It'll smell to high heaven, too."

"Never you mind," I said, and permitted myself the tiniest of wicked smiles. "I know what I'm doing."

And I did. Sort of.

Chapter 13

WHILE AT THE HIRYL I learned, among other things, how to take the hair off my legs with a cream that smelled like boiled skunk oil and how to buff my toenails until they gleamed like something you could get good money for. I was educated to select the right piece of silverware to use for which course—why, they had enough artillery on the table to start a revolution—and spent hours practicing on how to modulate my voice an octave lower than the lord intended it to be.

Then, about ten days after the business with the kitchen, some of the girls decided to go out and hunt snipes. Nancilee was sick upstairs with a headache, so I knew it'd be safe to go along. Snipes were little birds with long, skinny legs, DeLoris told me. They tasted sort of like squabs, she said.

"How do you fix 'em after you catch 'em?" I wanted to know. I liked roast squab the same way some people like chocolate cake, and I looked forward to sneaking into the park across the street from the HIRYL after we were supposed to be in bed and the snipes had come out to feed. Buster and Cash and I used to do some fishing; snipe hunting might be just as much fun.

I put on jeans and a shirt, but when DeLoris saw how I was dressed she said, "Hop back into your nightgown, Raella. It doesn't take a minute to catch snipes. We'll be back before you know it. You can hold the sack while the rest of us chase the little devils down your way.''

''What sack?''

''Well, we don't exactly have the right kind. You're supposed to have one with a drawstring. We'll just have to use a pillowcase and be sure to hold it tight shut after they crawl in. Why don't you take one off your pillow when you go up to change clothes?''

After I jumped back into my nightgown, I stripped the case from my pillow like DeLoris suggested and hurried downstairs. The lights were off because of course we didn't want to attract Mrs. Hayden's attention. I listened for the sound of Nancilee's voice in the darkness. If I heard it, I decided I'd quit the game then and there. Priscilla moved close to me and hooked her little finger with mine. ''Raella,'' she began, ''I don't think . . .''

''Shush, Priscilla, we got to get going,'' DeLoris broke in impatiently. ''See that tree right across the street, Raella?''

I told her I did. ''The one right to the near side of the sidewalk?'' I asked, just to be sure I had the right one.

''That's it, all right. Now you skip over there with your sack and wait for us. The rest of us'll be along in a jiff. We just don't want anyone to get suspicious, so we'll come one at a time.''

I zipped out. The sidewalk under my bare feet was chilly. I got to thinking about how many birds I knew that were night feeders. The only one that came quickly to mind was an owl. Maybe a snipe, even though it was small and long-legged, was a distant cousin to an owl. Granmaw Carmody always made cornbread stuffing for

103

squabs. I hoped when the cook at HIRYL roasted those snipes she'd fix them the way my granmaw fixed squab.

I heard the bolt slip in the door when it closed behind me. The girls didn't want any stranger bursting in on them, of course, while they stood in the front entry at a time when everyone was supposed to be upstairs asleep. I ran to the tree, ducked behind it, and waited. The HIRYL stayed dark and silent on the opposite side of the street.

When nobody came out after a few more minutes, I sort of waved my pillowcase at them to let everyone know I was ready. The door didn't open so much as a crack. I figured for sure Priscilla would be the next one out after me. "I'd like to come to Money Creek and visit you sometime," she'd said yesterday. I'd never imagined a girl like her would want to visit a girl like me. I told her it wouldn't be anything like boarding school. She told me that was why she wanted to come.

A policeman came up the walk, so I ducked behind the tree again and clutched my pillowcase tight to my chest. I wanted to catch some snipes, all right, but not get arrested in the process. After the sound of his footsteps vanished down the block, I hurried back across the street to see what was holding up the rest of the hunters. Just as I was about to rap softly on the door, I heard Nancilee Adams' voice on the other side of it.

"Did you ever in your life see such a *dunce*?" she was hooting. Other hoots accompanied hers. "Raella, dumbella! I can't believe anyone would fall for such an old, old joke!" Apparently she liked her money and her jokes both to be on the well-aged side.

I didn't raise the knocker, of course. I'd have stood out there in below-freezing weather and have turned into an icicle before I'd have asked any of them to let me inside. I hustled around to the side door, where I'd seen milk delivered in the morning. It was locked. I sat down near a shrub and folded my pillowcase around me as best I could.

By the time morning came I was so stiff and sore I could hardly move. I hadn't slept a wink either. I had plenty of time to think about my past. My future, too. I'd come to a few conclusions about each one of them. When cook opened the door a crack to reach for the milk, I jumped inside like a hungry cat. Blue Uniform was in the kitchen, getting his first cup of coffee for the day.

"You!" he snorted. "Might've known you'd be the kind to sneak out at night. Common, that's all you are. We've never had your sort at the Institute before. I don't know what Mrs. Hayden was thinking of when she let you apply. Common, that's all I can say."

"So's rainwater," I snapped, "but gooseberries don't grow without it." I dashed past him and up the back stairs. I had barely enough time to wash up and present myself at breakfast. Since it would be my last one at the HIRYL, I wanted to look calm, cool, and collected.

After we'd eaten and were upstairs brushing our teeth, Priscilla had a hard time looking me straight in the eye. "I didn't want to help them trick you, Raella," she apologized, "but . . . well, you know how Nancilee is. She got everyone to go along with it and I couldn't . . ."

"Hey, listen, don't worry," I said. "I knew all along they were going to lock me out." It was a lie. "Really, I did. Everybody had a good laugh. No harm done."

I took the top off my peanut butter jar. I stirred its contents with a knife I'd borrowed from the dining room. Darn! I'd gotten the chunky kind. But it was all ripe and rancid, just like Priscilla predicted. And since

105

it'd been extended with so much cottonseed oil, it was sort of soupy, too. Like I'd told Fronie her grits were. Great.

"I'd still like to visit you in Money Creek," Priscilla said as she watched me stir.

"Golly, you're welcome anytime," I said, and screwed the lid back on the jar. "Here, I'll write my address down for you." On a piece of paper I wrote: "E.R. Carmody, c/o The Diner, Money Creek, Missouri." Because very shortly, that's exactly where I was going to be.

It didn't take me long to pack my stuff that night after I was sure Priscilla was asleep. I gathered up the suitcase Maree had loaned me—it had her initials in gold on the handles—and got my peanut butter and my knife.

I eased myself into the hall. I set my suitcase down at the top of the stairs and tiptoed back to Nancilee's room. DeLoris had left the HIRYL that morning, still packing twenty too many pounds in her southern hemisphere, so I knew Nancilee was alone. I could hear her breathing on the other side of the door, regular and even. An uneasy conscience was not one of her problems: she was sleeping like a baby.

I opened the door and stepped quickly inside.

Nancilee slept with her window shade raised part way. Her cape of yellow hair was carefully arranged over her pillow. Very handy. I waited a long minute for her to stir, wake up, holler her fool head off to see me standing there. She snoozed blissfully on.

I took the cap off my jar of peanut butter. I stirred it with my knife. It smelled ripe as a catfish that's laid on a sandbank in the sun for a week.

And since it was cheap peanut butter, stretched with lots of cottonseed oil, it spread as easy as warm honey.

106

I decided to've gotten the chunky kind was not a bad mistake after all—it gave Nancilee's golden tresses a gritty, molten look like that piece of metal sculpture in St. Louis.

I stepped back to survey my artwork. Nancilee's hair was a glory to behold, all clotted together with peanut butter. I looked in the jar. I still had some left—enough to give her a nice peanut butter headband across her forehead. *Tormented Woman,* that piece at the museum had been called. Now she had a younger sister, *Miserable Girl,* lying sound asleep in Kentucky.

My job was done. I set the empty jar on Nancilee's dresser, laid the knife across its open mouth like a calling card. It was the classy sort of thing someone who'd been to finishing school would do.

I eased myself quietly out of her room, picked up my suitcase, closed the front door behind me, and hurried down the street. The bus left the station at five A.M. But before I got to the end of the block, I heard a scream that raised me six inches off the sidewalk. I turned back to the HIRYL. . . .

Nasty Nancilee's light was on and the window shade was still at half-mast. She was standing in front of the mirror over her dresser, one hand clapped to either side of her head. Her shrieks were the kind that would peel the plaster off a wall.

In another minute, every light in the place was on. I heard a security siren go off. Mrs. Hayden, followed by Blue Uniform and the cook, were pelting up the stairs. Girls had crowded into the hallway.

I hiked off down the street. A ground fog covered the whole city but already the morning sun was trying to peek through it. Everything was pearly, iridescent. It was good to be outdoors again. In Money Creek, horses

107

throughout the countryside would be stirring and stretching. Summer would be moving out of her shelter into the warm air. Was the foal inside her as big yet as a baby chicken? Or maybe a snipe, who was not a cousin to an owl?

I shifted my suitcase from one hand to the other. I was going home. To Money Creek, where I belonged. I wondered if it would ever dawn on Nancilee Adams that to a certain Missouri girl, old money didn't smell one bit better than cheap peanut butter.

Chapter 14

IT WAS LATE afternoon before I found myself walking up the white road between the twin rows of oak and willow that led to Fairfield Farms. I found Denis and Maree drinking their after-lunch coffee on the flagstone patio at the back of the house. It didn't seem like summer should've been ending so soon, but a few yellow leaves skipped across the stones with an autumn sound as I approached.

Naturally Denis and Maree were astonished to see me. They'd been sure I was safe over there in Kentucky, getting finished and polished the same way Old Man Evans polishes the pretty rocks he finds along Money Creek. To see me standing there in front of them, my rough edges still showing, was quite a shock. But I could tell by their welcome they had not yet gotten a phone call from Mrs. Hayden, which would make my job a lot easier.

"Good heavens!" Denis exclaimed. "You must have a twin, Raella. It can't be our own girl who stands before us."

"One and the same," I told him. "Come back to Money Creek where she belongs."

Maree was silent and I fancied there was something like fear in her eyes. Then she bustled about seeing to it that Helga got some lunch for me. First, though, she said she wanted me to come upstairs. There was something I just had to see. . . .

Pooki did not miss the chance to sew a few red threads on my ankle as I followed Maree up the stairs. The door of my room was shut. "We wanted to do something special for you, Raella," Maree said. "Close your eyes now and don't open them until I tell you to."

I obeyed, and heard her open the bedroom door. She took me by the hand and led me through it. "Now— look!" I opened my eyes and discovered I'd waded into a lemon pie. The whole room—which had been lovely enough before—had been redone in yellow and white. The wallpaper boasted great chains of yellow roses tied with yellow ribbons, the bedspread was yellow organdy, the curtains at the window were white and frothy as meringue.

"Isn't it pretty, Raella? Oh, I think it's just like you—fresh and radiant and so . . . *you*!" The idea made her so happy she put an arm around my shoulder and squeezed me.

"Oh, Maree, I don't think . . ."

"No, no, Raella," she soothed, thinking she understood my problem. "Don't be a bit embarrassed. We *wanted* to do it for you. Don't worry about thanking us. You've brought so much pleasure into our lives. Just filled it up, that's what you've done. But come along now—I'm sure Helga has got something ready for you to eat."

The scrambled egg sandwich Helga made for me was tasty, but knowing what I had to tell the Puckett-Smythes made it hard to eat. Then I had to polish off a piece of strawberry shortcake. When at last I was finished, we three faced each other around the table and listened to the wind stir the flowers in the garden. Some of the early bloomers had begun to brown and the sigh of the wind along their crisp edges was mournful to my ears.

"I guess you're probably wondering why I came back so sudden," I said. They both watched me. That wary, lonesome look sneaked back into Maree's blue eyes. I wondered if she'd been through this sort of thing before—of wanting to love and be loved by a person who couldn't. I decided maybe that was what had happened to Rosanne and Cash, too. Trying to make people into persons they were never meant to be is a risky business.

I swallowed a couple times. I tried to frame the words in my mind. I wanted to be as nice about it as I could manage to be. "I don't believe I'm quite the girl you had in mind," I began. "I mean, I wanted to be, to make up for what I'd done. Maybe if you'd caught me sooner there might've been some hope."

Neither of them stirred. They waited for me to go on.

"I'm too much of a Carmody, that's the whole problem," I explained. "My roots just go too deep. To've gotten rid of them would've been the same kind of hard work Granpaw Carmody faced when he tried to grub out those oak stumps on his place, you know? Such hard work."

"I . . . we both hoped . . . that somehow . . ." Maree began, then her voice trailed off, thin and wispy as smoke. She couldn't finish. She didn't cry. She started to shuffle the plates and glasses around the table, brushed crumbs off into her palm, held them there, gazed away into the afternoon distance. Behind her clear eyes there was a sadness I did not want to look at too long.

I cleared my throat again. "Of course," I admitted,

"that still leaves us with the little matter about how I stole Dark Victory's services. I've got an idea, though, if you'd like to hear it."

Denis gave me a wan smile. "Ideas do not seem to be a commodity you ever run short of, Raella."

"Maybe that colt our red mare will drop next May will turn out to be the fastest foal in four counties," I said. "It could be. You just can't tell about some things. Might be one of the greatest Dark Victory ever sired. Whatever kind it is, though, it's your property. Soon's that foal is weaned, I think you ought to take possession of it. It's the only fair thing. On its mama's side its lines will go all the way back to Man o' War. If you don't want to keep the colt, you can always sell it for a handsome price."

Neither Denis nor Maree said a word. I figured I'd taken the wrong tack completely. There *was* one other solution, of course. "On the other hand," I reminded them, "you can charge me with grand larceny. Which is okay. Really. I mean, what I did was a crime and I know it."

Denis laid his hands palm down on the table and inspected his fingernails like he hadn't seen them in a long while. "There are lots of different kinds of crime in this world, Raella," he sighed. "Maybe Maree and I made our own pact with the devil when we tried to make a bargain with you." It sounded like something Granmaw Carmody would say. "But it didn't work out, that's all. Life is like that sometimes."

He stroked his chin. He seemed tired all of a sudden. "I will speak to our lawyer tomorrow. We will try to work out some sort of agreement that is fair to all of us." He studied me for a moment. "And I expect Maree and I had best forget anything as formal as . . .

112

as adoption proceedings, hadn't we?" So Mrs. Hayden had known what she was talking about after all. . . .

Maree stared past both of us, out toward the paddock where she and I had seen Dark Victory the first morning we spent together. "My goodness, autumn seems to be coming early this year," she murmured. She shivered and hugged herself with both arms.

Her face had lost the softness that'd been stealing over it during the weeks I'd known her. Once again it was smooth as marble. Then, with her light and brittle laugh, she suggested to me, "Ella Rae, why don't you run upstairs and pack your things? If you hurry, you can be home before dark." As suddenly as she started to love me, she stopped. I wondered if that's what happened to that little boy in Italy, too.

One thing for sure—I knew what *we* had was over. Not because she told me to go upstairs and pack. Because she took back the name Raella. Now it belonged to that girl who'd never been a real person anyway. I was plain old Ella Rae Carmody again, who had come to Fairfield Farms to be household help. Female preferred.

But she was right about one thing: it didn't take me long to pack. I didn't carry away a single thing I hadn't come with. I left behind all the shirts and sweaters and the towels with initials that didn't match the person I really was. I could get everything I owned into one paper grocery sack.

Maree was gone from the table on the patio when I came downstairs to say good-bye. Denis' gray eyes were calm and didn't accuse me of anything. He hung onto my hand a little longer than was necessary. "It was nice to have you here this summer, Ella Rae," he said.

All of a sudden, I knew why I'd always liked him. I decided to tell him the reason.

"You're just like me, Mr. Puckett-Smythe," I said.

The good news caught him off guard. "How do you mean?" he asked, as if he wasn't sure he really wanted to know.

"You wanted to do for Maree—Mrs. Puckett-Smythe, I mean—the same thing I wanted to do for Cash. You wanted to make her happy, that's all. I tried to get a foal for my daddy's red mare and you tried to catch . . ."

". . . a daughter for my wife," he finished for me. The word "daughter" was hardly out of his mouth before his eyes got misty. "We almost adopted a child once before," he admitted, fidgeting with my fingers as he spoke. "We lived in Italy at the time. The lad was charming, big brown eyes and all, but shortly after he arrived he became ill. The villa in France was unfortunate, too, because it turned out the foundations were unsound and required huge sums to be put aright. Maree, you see, didn't want anything . . ."

". . . that wasn't perfect." It was my turn to finish for him. I had tidy eyebrows, holes in my ears, and a few weeks at finishing school to prove it.

Mr. Puckett-Smythe nodded, gave my fingers one last squeeze, then turned them loose. He wanted to say something else but couldn't find the right words. So I told him good-bye the best way I knew.

"My Granmaw Carmody would've liked you, sir. She would've said you are a good scout."

I hiked off down the road toward Money Creek, my paper sack snuggled under my arm. But I turned to look back one final time.

Mrs. Puckett-Smythe was standing in her empty lemon-pie room. She held the frothy curtain away from the

114

window and watched me walk out of her life. I wished I could've told her what I knew about love—that it's hardly ever the way you think it ought to be. It was too late for that. Instead, I put my fingers to my lips and blew her a farewell kiss.

But she was like Rosanne—she couldn't blow one back to me.

Chapter 15

OAT SNEPP was the very first person I laid eyes on that afternoon when I walked into Money Creek from the altitudes of Fairfield Farms.

"Where you been, Bones?" he wanted to know. "I haven't seen hide or hair of you all summer long. You learn any of those magic tricks like you wanted?"

He had remembered. But I shook my head. "They turned out to be a whole lot harder to do than I ever counted on," I said.

Oat slowed his orange ten-speed and walked it along beside me. He revved the handle grip a few times like it was connected to a motor, which I could plainly see it was not. "Gramps hung up his helmet," Oat told me. "Said he still loved life in the fast lane but it was time to give the younger fellas a chance." He paused and seemed to have something else he wanted to say.

"You want to go down to your Uncle Waldo's and split a Pepsi with me?" he asked. "He's got a new pop machine; maybe you haven't seen it yet. Put it right out there on the sidewalk in front of the store. Got him some benches, too. The machine is nice. Green and white. Push a button, you get extra ice if you want it." Well, Waldo had always been a man with a good head for business.

"Can't manage it today, Oat," I said. I noticed his eyes were a pretty golden brown, about the same color as water running over fallen maple leaves in Money Creek, a fact I'd never taken account of before. "I guess I'll have to take a rain check."

"Rain check? That mean we can maybe go later?"

"That's what it means, all right," I said. I hadn't known myself until Nasty Nancilee laid the information on me. "Right now, Oat, I've got to check on my family. What's left of it, that is." What I didn't tell him was that I hoped we could all be a tribe again. Some-way; somehow.

I didn't walk straight up to The Diner. First, I stopped off to see Summer. She didn't seem at all surprised to see me, and came right to the fence when I called her. "How you been, girl?" I asked, and rubbed her red ears. I took a peek at her sides: they were filling out already. She looked sleek and happy. I smelled my fingers. Once again they were covered with the rich, sweet, earthy smell of horse. I knew for sure I was home.

But The Diner I found was not the same one I'd left. The dogearred card in the window read "Open," and it was, too. Through the windows—which had been freshly washed and didn't complain of a single flyspeck—I counted six people, all eating and talking back and forth, acting like they were real happy to be there. My red-and-white-checkered curtains had been newly washed and ironed. And there, presiding behind the counter that used to be mine, like a queen before her court but not pound thinner, was Fronie.

She nearly spilled the cup of coffee she was
when I walked in. "Why, Ella Rae, I declare

heard a word from you all the time you were gone, hon. You back to stay?''

"Yes, ma'am," I said. At that news, she looked nervous and her cup chattered against its saucer when she set it down.

"Don't worry about it, Fronie. We'll manage to get along somehow. I don't know how exactly, but we'll work on it.''

"Speaking of working on things, hon, we been working on getting Buster and Chloe back. It just kills your daddy not to have 'em underfoot.'' When she spoke she didn't look at me in the fond and loving way Mrs. Puckett-Smythe used to. Fronie just looked right straight at me. Saw me warts and all. It didn't seem to bother her, either. I knew she'd never try to invent another me; it wasn't in her nature. "Cash missed you, too, hon. More than he liked to let on.''

"How come you're getting the kids back?" I asked. "I mean, how much ransom did you have to pay?" Fronie smiled and shrugged a plump shoulder. "Well, there *was* a price," she admitted shyly. "I better tell you that right off." She looked down and began to wash the counter that was already spotless.

I waited. She waited. She cleared her throat just like I had when I tried to tell the Puckett-Smythes something they didn't want to hear. "If . . . if we get the right kind of atmosphere back in here, I guess Buster and Chloe can come home again.''

I figured I knew what she meant. "You mean you and Cash got to get married, right?''

She nodded. "Did Cash and Rosanne get divorced vhile I was gone?" I hated to say that word: *divorced*. ght from the minute Rosanne flew out of the yard that afternoon with her truckload of feathered friends, I'd been hoping she'd come back. But she hadn't even written. Not once a week. Not at all.

"No, they aren't divorced," Fronie admitted softly. "Not yet. Cash can't seem to locate your mama so's he can get the papers served on her. She never answers any of the mail he sends either." As she spoke, Cash himself wheeled into the yard. I looked at the clock on the wall. Only five-thirty. Fronie saw my glance. "He's home nearly almost every night," she said proudly. "He wants to be a family again just as much as you, hon."

Fronie fixed us some chicken-fried steak for supper that night, with mountains of mashed potatoes and pools of pan gravy. I couldn't have done better myself. I decided she'd probably cook spinach the right way, too. Wouldn't thrash it to death in a blender, then throw nutmeg and cream all over it to cover up the damage she'd done.

Cash squeezed my hand twice across the table. His eyes were as clear as a child's. "It's so good to have you back where you belong, girl," he told me. "Now all we got to do is get those little ones back too."

"Can't we kidnap them back?"

Cash shook a finger under my nose. "You ought to've learned by now, Ella Rae, those sorts of ideas have a way of going badly astray. I'm hoping we can work out an arrangement for temporary custody. We'll get the permanent kind as soon . . . as soon as Fronie and I get married. Aunt Bea even signed a paper testifying we're decent folks."

"Then why'd she turn traitor on you in the place?" I groused.

119

"I think it was because she was upset about Rosanne. It was her sister ran off, remember. Left her children high and dry. I think Bea was embarrassed. With Waldo McFee being such a big man in town, Bea decided to take it all out on Fronie."

When Cash went off to work the next morning, and after Fronie opened The Diner and started a batch of French toast for some folks on vacation from Arkansas, she sent me down to the courthouse to get some release papers from Miss Rowe. Miss Rowe, who'd driven the getaway car with Buster and Chloe inside it, turned out to be a lady who wouldn't think twice about rapping you smartly on the knuckles with a steel-edged ruler if you didn't behave just so.

"Well," she began sourly, "so you're the one who got in all that trouble with the owners of Fairfield Farms. It's people like you give this community a bad name."

But I had not been sent to finishing school for nothing. I lowered myself smoothly into a chair. I crossed my ankles but not my knees. I rested one elbow on the corner of her desk. I set myself to give her a good dose of some jungle grace.

"I regret that you have been so seriously misinformed, my dear Miss Rowe," I purred. "Why, only yesterday I lunched with Mr. and Mrs. Puckett-Smythe on the terrace at Fairfield Farms. They told me I am someone they will not soon forget."

Miss Rowe watched me with a narrowed eye, so I dropped my voice an octave lower than the lord intended it to be and went right on:

"My father says temporary custody might be arranged for my brother, Elvis Presley Carmody, aged six, and

120

for my sister, Chloe Rosanne Carmody, aged almost three. You see, Miss Rowe, my father plans to be married again soon, and he'd like the little ones home so they can share in the new life we all plan to take up."

"This is terribly unusual," Miss Rowe complained. "I don't think I have the authority. . . . I mean, no one has ever asked . . . I think I should check with Mr. Hamacher." She leaped up from her desk like I'd walked into the place with a gun and disappeared into an office made of frosted glass on the opposite side of the room. Minutes later, a man came out to inspect me.

"You are the eldest Carmody child?" he asked. He was balding and pink and had smooth pink hands like an opossum. It was my turn to inspect him. I did so with a superior gaze. Such looks had worked so well for Pooki and Nancilee. I left my ankles crossed.

"Correct, sir," I said. "I haven't been around town much this summer, on account of I just got back from spending a few wonderful weeks at the Hayden Institute for the Refinement of Young Ladies."

"The HIRYL!" Mr. Hamacher exclaimed, as impressed as he could be. "Why, my sister's daughters— my sister is married to a brain surgeon in Bangor, Maine—went there, too! Betsy and Polly said they had some unforgettable experiences at the Institute."

"Yes, sir," I agreed, "some folks have unforgettable experiences there, all right." I could think of at least one person who had and her initials were N.A.

Mr. Hamacher pressed his pink, possum hands together. "About your brother and sister, Miss Carmody. I am sure we can work out an arrangement for temporary custody. . . ."

121

He was a man of his word, and when I left the courthouse that afternoon with some release papers, even Miss Rowe was able to crack out a smile. I skipped right over to the Branches to collect Buster.

Chapter 16

I FOUND Buster alone in the front yard of the Branches' house, which was hemmed in by a tidy white picket fence covered with purple clematis. As usual, Buster was not slow to speak his mind the minute he laid eyes on me.

"What'd you send me a postcard for, Ella Rae? You know I can't read. Mrs. Branch had to tell me what it said."

"I forgot, Buster. Sometimes you seem older to me than you really are." That seemed to please him. He almost smiled. I noticed that he was not wearing his glasses. "What happened to your specs, Buster?"

He touched his face quickly as though he'd only recently given up wearing them and still missed their weight on the bridge of his nose. "I just turned loose of 'em about three days ago," he admitted. "Mrs. Branch said they were childish. She decided to call me Elvis, too."

"Well, Elvis, let's get on over to pick up Chloe."

"Chloe who? I don't know anyone named Chloe."

"Of course you do. Chloe is your sister, dopus." We were slipping easily, happily back into our old contentious habits. Full of sibling rivalry. They felt comfortable. I could see from the look on Elvis' face he thought they were comfortable, too.

"Mrs. Branch said I was abandoned. Everybody else said so, too. That's like being an orphan."

"You weren't abandoned, Elvis. Misplaced, maybe, but not ever abandoned." He seemed glad to have me put the whole thing in focus for him. He reached for my hand. I showed the release papers to Mrs. Branch and she said she'd miss my brother. "He's a nice little boy but an awful picky eater," she said. That's the truth, I told her. Been that way as long as I can remember.

Chloe was on the front porch of her foster home, which was located up the street and to the left of the OK Hardware Store, at the Perkins'. She was wearing a pink dress. I hadn't seen Chloe in a dress since she was six months old and we'd had her baptized. She studied Elvis and me for a long minute and then smiled Cash's wide, glad smile. Her teeth were small, square, and perfect.

"Hi, Buster," she said. "Hi, Ella Rae."

"Chloe! You can talk!"

"Sure," she said. "Are we going home now?"

I bent down and scooped her into my arms. Her pants were pink to match her dress. They were dry, too. I couldn't wait to tell old money-in-the-bank Waldo McFee he'd been wrong about Chloe's oars. She had both of them in the water now.

As we three marched home, holding hands, me in the middle and the little ones on either side, we came upon Aunt Bea. I scowled. She'd been a traitor to us.

"Goodness, Ella Rae," she said, "don't look at me that way. Makes me wonder if you got an upset stomach and need some soda."

"Well, what you did causes me to get a little sick, that's a fact," I said.

Aunt Bea's hair was still in rollers. I wondered if

124

she'd worn them ever since I left for Fairfield Farms. "I never meant to make bad trouble for anyone," she sighed. "I guess I was upset over what Rosanne did. Blamed all the wrong people. Hasn't that ever happened to you, Ella Rae?"

"Never," I lied. "Have you heard from Rosanne?"

"Hardly a word. Not since right after she left and told me she had a friend."

"A friend?"

"She said his name was Billy." *A new life*, Fronie had called it. *Lots of times it means a fella*. It was not a subject I cared to think about.

A week later, *The Money Creek News*, which had helped launch me on a life of crime in the first place, devoted their entire issue to an event that rocked our whole town: Fairfield Farms had been sold.

The picture taken of Mr. and Mrs. Puckett-Smythe, as they boarded a plane in St. Louis, was fuzzy as usual. Maree wore dark glasses and carried Pooki in a wicker basket. Denis' face looked naked, for he'd shaved off his handsome mustache. Behind them, I could see a scowl that belonged to Helga. Grady Myers was staying on at the farm to help its new owners take charge. "The former proud possessors of Dark Victory," the rest of us were told, "will soon make their home in London, England, where they formerly traveled and still have many famous friends."

Famous friends. But no child. No daughter halfway between a filly with possibilities and a real person. Maree must've tossed out her wish to be a Famous Mother of the South. "*The world is mine*," she'd read to me from Edna St. Vincent Millay: "*Broad field, bright flower, and long white road . . .*" She'd had all those things, too. She'd wanted roots as much as me, but wouldn't hang around long enough to let some get a good deep start.

Now if she'd stayed in Money Creek, maybe we could all have been friends. She could've met Elvis and Chloe. At long last it was even safe to hold Chloe on your lap. But Mrs. Puckett-Smythe had a passion for turning horses and houses and children into works of perfection. She couldn't be content with anything that fell short of what she had in mind.

After they were gone, the Puckett-Smythes' lawyer sent me a letter. "Re: Denis and Maree Puckett-Smythe vs. Ella Rae Carmody," was how he described the problem. "When the foal sired by Dark Victory, whether it be stud foal or filly, has reached the age of six months and/or been weaned from its dam [the red mare known as 'Summer'], said foal shall be relinquished to its rightful owners, Denis and Maree Puckett-Smythe, who will subsequently offer said foal for sale at public auction."

Well, so much for that, I figured. Then I read on:

"In the event, however, that Ella Rae Carmody or her guardians are able to pay the stated sum of $3,000—or the advertised fee for acquisition of Dark Victory's service prior to the weaning of said foal—such animal shall be remanded to the custody of the Carmody family."

"Does that mean we can keep the colt?" I asked Cash.

"That's what it means, all right," he said. "But three thousand dollars is still three thousand dollars, Ella Rae."

Just the same, the Puckett-Smythes had cared enough

about me to leave the door open a crack. To give us Carmodys some hope. It was all I needed. Why, if I thought about it long enough, I might get an idea. It would probably come suddenly. My best ones usually did.

Chapter 17

ONCE I THOUGHT owning a mare named Summer, who'd throw the Carmodys colts that would trace their ancestors all the way back to Man o' War, might make summer itself last forever. It didn't, of course.

What I never imagined, though, was that its last days would bring Rosanne back to Money Creek.

Oh, she hadn't come to stay, she was quick to tell me. It was lucky, she added, she'd got there when I was the only person at The Diner. She hadn't let Elvis and Chloe tell her good-bye. Now she didn't want them to say hello. She didn't even know that Buster wasn't Buster anymore.

But she didn't wheel back into the yard in any old blue truck loaded with chickens, I'll say that for her. She came in a low-slung, sassy little red sportscar with lots of chrome on it and a black leather folding top. Hadn't she told me red was the color of life? But for a minute, when that car pulled up in front of The Diner, I couldn't imagine who had stopped. Didn't know, even when she stepped inside the door, who in the world it could be.

"Why, Rosanne," I said, after she took off a pair of sunglasses that were mirrored and big as dinner plates, "it's you. You've come back. . . ."

She wiggled a long red nail under my nose. "Not to stay, Babe, not to stay," she assured me gaily. "I'm only passing through on my way to someplace more interesting."

"You never wrote like you said you would, Rosanne."

"Oh, I know I didn't, Babe. My intentions were good but I got so busy, see? I wrote to Beatrice, though. Didn't she tell you?" I wondered what she could've said that would make Aunt Bea turn traitor on us. "Bea allowed to me all of you were coming along just swell without me. Besides, Babe, I knew you were a take-charge kind of kid. Always were. So old! You never needed much looking after."

The Puckett-Smythes had wanted to look after me in the worst way, but I hadn't been able to let them. *Old.* The way Rosanne said the word made me wince. As if it were somehow hateful. Something she never wanted to be. I decided not to tell her about Mrs. Hayden's Scotch tape. I peeked around her, out to the car parked in front of The Diner. "Who's that you got with you, Rosanne? Is he the fella named Billy that I heard about?"

"Billy? You heard about Billy? Well, yes; that's him. Billy is my . . . my friend."

"Oh." I nodded and wiped invisible crumbs off the counter just like Fronie did when she didn't know what to say after I came home. "That's nice, Rosanne. Cash has got himself a friend, too. Her name's Fronie."

Rosanne colored up pink as her name when I said that. She didn't want me to think she and Billy were the same kind of friends to one another as Cash and Fronie were. Wanted me to believe for her it was different. Better. But to see her look so stricken and pink wasn't going to help anybody, so I said, "Hey, Rosanne, don't fret about it. It's okay. I understand. Really. I do."

This time, it was the truth. "I'll be sixteen in two more weeks, remember?"

But she was hardly paying me any attention at all. She was restless and roamed the length of the counter. She had something on her mind. Finally she said: "Somehow, I don't know why, I thought maybe when I came back you'd call me mama."

Why had such a notion taken hold of her? She didn't even mean to stay. "Wouldn't it sound strange to both of us, Rosanne? I mean, as long as we've known each other you've been Rosanne to me. You know that."

"Do you call *her* mama?" She meant Fronie.

"Gosh, no, Rosanne. I don't call Fronie mama, because she isn't, among other things. She's just Fronie to all of us. Even Chloe. She's a good person, Fronie is. Fluffy and soft as a feather bed. I think you might even like her."

"I doubt it, Babe."

"Why not? You don't even know her yet, Rosanne."

Rosanne began to fuss needlessly at the neck of her dress with her long red nails. I snatched a look at her; she looked a good deal different than when she'd left. She'd always been a person made of angles, corners, and points. Now she was more so. Mrs. Eustachia Hayden would've been crazy about her. But her hair was an alarm. It used to be her pride and joy. She loved it when somebody came into The Diner and hollered, "Hiya, Goldilocks!" Now its gold was brighter and harder, the same color as that picture frame I got at the fair in Chilhowee that later turned such a queer shade of green.

The Diner had gotten hot and stuffy. There was no way I could clean the counter cleaner than it already was. I hung up the washcloth and said, "Let's go over to the paddock, Rosanne. I got something nice to show you.'' We moved out the back door and took the cinder path that led to the paddock. The sign we'd put up, Money Creek Farms, Inc., looked so businesslike in the later summer sun. Rosanne studied it for a moment but gave me no hint as to what she thought about it.

"Do you like it out there in California?" I asked, trying to poke some life back into our conversation.

It took her a minute to answer. "Sure, Babe. I like it fine. It's where I always wanted to go, remember?"

"Did you get a job right away like you planned?" I had to ask all the questions she'd never answered in all those letters she never wrote.

"Found one straightaway. It wasn't hard at all."

"What doing?" It probably made her so proud. Like she hadn't made a terrible mistake at all. Maybe she worked in a movie studio. Was a secretary to some big director. Or escorted visitors around film sets, explaining about how pictures are made, all dressed up in a navy uniform with brass buttons, waiting for some producer to discover her and put her in a movie.

"I work in a diner, Babe."

"A . . . *diner* . . . ?"

"It isn't much different from this one, Babe. Oh, lots more folks drop by, of course. We're busy nearly all of the time. But you still got to keep the sugar bowls filled. Got to hustle for a tip. We have a palm tree right outside the door, though."

"You seen any movie stars yet?"

"I saw Danny Desmond. Remember, he was in that show *Summer and Sin*, the one we saw at the drive-in? Yes, I saw him. He was across the street. In a car. He was headed in the opposite direction. But I could see right off it was Danny Desmond."

There had been a question I'd planned to ask her. Had tried it out on the water spots on the ceiling of the bedroom when I was sure Elvis and Chloe were asleep. Had worded it a dozen different ways.

Have you ever been sorry you traded all your Monday Creek yesterdays for a California tomorrow? I decided I didn't really need to hear her answer.

Summer moved from her shed into a patch of soft, last-of-summer sunshine. "She's still mighty pigeon-toed, isn't she?" Rosanne remarked with a frown.

"That's a fact," I admitted. "On the other hand, doesn't the rest of her look fine? She's in the family way, you know. Going to have her first colt next spring. We bred her to Dark Victory from Fairfield Farms, just like Cash wanted." I wished she'd had time to hear the whole story. I'd liked to have thought she wanted to listen. "I've already named the foal, too. Summer Victory, after each one of its parents."

"You and Cash," Rosanne sighed. "Still dreaming your same dreams."

The minute she spoke of dreams and dreaming, the air between us went damp and soggy again. Rosanne had run out of comments to make. I'd run out of questions to ask.

But there was one small thing I wanted her to know before she left Money Creek a second time—knowing, as I did, that it might be a while before I saw her again. "Sometimes, Rosanne," I said, "I go back down to Racker's Mill. I look at that quilt of purple flowers. They're through blooming for the year. I think about when you and Cash were young. Thanks, Rosanne. I'm glad you told me."

She turned to stare at me, as shy and startled as any woods' creature you might flush out of a hawthorne thicket. "Oh, Babe . . . it wasn't much you ever asked for, was it?" That knowledge caused a bruised sound to creep into her voice. The look on her face was the same one as on Mrs. Puckett-Smythes' when I told her I was not the child she had in mind.

Another wonderful idea came to me. "Say, Rosanne! How'd you like it if I came out to see you sometime? Out there in California? Next summer, maybe, after the Money Creek colt has been born? How'd you like that, Rosanne?" I laid my hand over one of hers on the top rail of the paddock fence.

She turned away from me, hiked one shoulder up, tucked her amazing yellow head down the way a bird will do when the wind is cold. She did not want me to see her cry. When she turned back to me, she gave me a clumsy, left-handed hug.

"Sure, Babe. I'd like that. Really. I would." Her voice was warm and chokey. "I'll write to you and send you that ticket just like I promised. We'll have ourselves a good time. You'll see. I won't forget, Babe."

Then she was gone, up the cinder path to the parking lot in front of The Diner where her friend Billy waited in his little red car. In she jumped; Billy turned a wheelie in the dust, and down the road they flew. When they got to the corner, they spurted up the road toward St. Louis like a bar of soap along a shower floor, just like when Rosanne had escaped that first time. She held up a long white arm.

"See you, Babe!" came her farewell cry.

Babe. My mother was the only person ever to call me that name—my mother, Rosanne Carmody—who along with me wasn't sure I'd ever been one.

Chapter 18

CASH AND FRONIE didn't linger as long in Libertyville as I figured they might. They were getting the divorce papers all lined up so they could send them to Rosanne. Fronie came home loaded with goodies for everyone—stuff to make hush puppies for Elvis and Chloe; chocolate-covered cherries for Cash; a nice notebook with a plastic cover that looked like real leather for me, to keep records on Summer's first motherhood.

I didn't want to tell them right away about Rosanne. But I couldn't get her off my mind.

"Gosh, you'll never guess who stopped by The Diner today," I finally said. Neither Cash or Fronie paid me much attention. "Rosanne, that's who." Cash darted a scared look at Fronie. She threw a frantic one back his way.

"Well. How was she?" Fronie managed to say as soon as she got her breath. "Back in Money Creek to stay, is she?"

"My, no," I said. "She's already taken herself another hike down the road." Both Cash and Fronie seemed relieved at that piece of news. "She said she was only passing through on her way to someplace more interesting." I gave Cash the slip of paper Rosanne left with her address on it.

134

"A pity Elvis and Chloe couldn't have seen her, too," Fronie said.

"Fronie, I don't think Rosanne wanted 'em to see her."

"Oh. Maybe it's best that way, come to think of it. How about you? You have a nice visit with your mother?"

Your mother. Those two words chased each other sadly through my heart. She would always be my mother. I would always be her daughter. Why hadn't we ever felt glad about it? "Fronie, Rosanne is Rosanne," I said. "Just like you're Fronie. Sometimes I feel like I never had a mother at all. I feel like I was hatched."

"Maybe there's worse things in this world."

"Name one, please. Just one."

"Not being hatched at all. Maybe that's worse." She paused by the table, ate another hush puppy, gave my shoulder an amiable squeeze. I knew then why it was that Chloe liked to lay in her lap, curled and content as a cat full of cream.

All through supper, Cash kept his thoughts to himself. Afterward, when I got ready to check on Summer one last time before going to bed myself, Cash decided he'd go along with me. To fork down some hay, he said. Help me out a little. I knew it wasn't his real reason.

"Ella Rae," he said, when we got outside The Diner, "there's something I been meaning to talk to you about." His voice was hesitant, like when he asked me how Summer'd got bred, when he wasn't sure he wanted to hear the answers.

"Fire away, Cash," I said. "The air's full of pigeons."

"Fronie and I got those divorce papers all fixed up today," he went on. "Soon's Rosanne agrees, the deed will be done. It'll be all over and finished between your mama and me. Then I expect Fronie and I will get married.''

"I expect so," I said.

The shadows behind Summer's shelter were dark. The days were already getting shorter. I knew Cash had to say what he did—but I didn't want to hear the word: *divorce*. I'd hoped so much Rosanne would come home to stay. Be a real mother. Underneath, I wasn't so different from Mrs. Puckett-Smythe—I wanted life to be a certain way.

"I know how you feel, Ella Rae. I know you love your mama just like you love me. I know it hurts." Never in my life had I admitted when I hurt. Now it was my turn to tuck my head under my wing so no one could see my tears. Cash took it the wrong way, though.

"I thought . . . I guess Fronie sort of hoped . . . well, I want you to like her, Ella Rae. She's been good to the little ones and . . ."

"Oh, I like her okay," I sniffled. It was true. Maybe not as much as Elvis and Chloe, but that might change in time. "And since when have I ever complained about anything?"

"You're just like your Granmaw Carmody. Now didn't she have a lot of starch in her drawers! Never complained. I liked her for that. I like you for it, too." He hugged me hard. Such riches! Two whole hugs in one day. But I was ready to live with such wealth.

"Come on, Ella Rae. Let's go back to The Diner," he urged. "Summer's all set for the night. Fronie's going to dish up some ice cream for the little ones. You come have a dish, too." I knew he didn't want to leave me alone with my mournful feelings.

But sometimes you have to have a little time for that.

136

"Cash, it's okay." I sniffled again. "Really. You go on and I'll be along in a minute. Really. Now—git!" I gave him a teary-eyed swat.

He left and I finished rubbing Summer down. She smelled rich, and her body under my hands was warm and full of life. Yes, her sides were definitely filling out. She had a becalmed look about her. In the dim light of the shed you couldn't even tell she was pigeon-toed. She looked like what she was: a handsome red mare who could trace her ancestors all the way back to Man o' War.

Above the open half-door, the moon was pumpkin-colored and as pregnant as our mare. Priscilla hadn't bothered to write to me. She called on the phone instead. "Can I still come to see you sometime?" she wanted to know. "Sure, love to have you," I said. "By the way," she told me, "it took Nancilee two days and sixteen shampoos to get all that yukky peanut butter out of her hair."

I closed the top half of the shed door, left our mare alone with her foal growing inside her. The fireflies should've been long gone for the year, but one of summer's lone survivors blinked past the end of my nose and vanished into the night. I considered the purple flowers that grew at Racker's Mill. Thought about visiting Rosanne in California. Wondered when Cash and Fronie would get married.

Then I wished for Ella Rae Carmody the nicest thing I could think of.

"Ella Rae, may all your tickets be the two-way kind." I'd go to California, sure enough. But I'd come back. I touched the edge of our new sign: Money Creek Farms, Inc. Home of a red mare that'd give the Carmodys a long line of fast, fleet colts. Home of Ella Rae Carmody.

Through a window of The Diner I watched Fronie dish up some ice cream. I started up the cinder path. I saw a flash of orange in the dusk and Oat Snepp wheeled past. "Want to meet me at your Uncle Waldo's tomorrow, Bones?" he called over his shoulder.

"Why not?" I hollered back. Of course, I was going to be awfully busy tomorrow. I had to start thinking about how us Carmodys could save up three thousand dollars so we wouldn't have to give up Summer's foal. The cinders under my feet were crisp. Overhead, the soft Missouri sky covered me like an umbrella. Under it, all my Carmody ancestors were spread like roots from a tree. *Granmaw,* I whispered into the twilit air, *I got my soul back.*

Summer was over. I walked into The Diner to eat ice cream with the rest of my tribe. Fronie included.

ABOUT THE AUTHOR

Patricia Calvert, who lives in Chatfield, Minnesota, is a senior editorial assistant in the Section of Publications of the Mayo Clinic. She holds a degree in history and is working toward a master's degree in children's literature. Her first novel, *THE SNOWBIRD*, is also available in a Signet Vista edition.